# THE GUNSMITH

# 469

# The Tall Texan

**Books by J.R. Roberts**
**(Robert J. Randisi)**

*The Gunsmith* series

*Gunsmith Giant* series

*Lady Gunsmith* series

*Angel Eyes* series

*Tracker* series

*Mountain Jack Pike* series

**COMING SOON!**
**The Gunsmith**
470 – Gunsmith for Hire

**For more information visit:**
www.SpeakingVolumes.us

# THE GUNSMITH

# 469

# **The Tall Texan**

J.R. Roberts

SPEAKING VOLUMES, LLC
NAPLES, FLORIDA
2021

The Tall Texan

ISBN 978-1-64540-451-4

# Chapter One

He was known as The Tall Texan.

He was called that because nobody knew his name, and—from all reports—he was more than six-and-a-half feet tall.

He had become a legend, pulling jobs all over the Southwest with no specialty. He had robbed trains, stagecoaches, banks, payrolls. Nobody had ever seen his face, he usually worked alone, and he had never killed anyone. Women he had robbed said he was a complete gentleman. He started his career in Texas, and then fanned out. He had been hunted by county sheriffs, town marshals, bounty hunters, U.S. marshals and hired guns.

When the file came across Robert Pinkerton's San Francisco desk, he immediately thought the best man to send after a legend would be a legend.

He called his secretary into his office and said, "Get this telegram off right away."

"Where to, sir?"

"Everywhere!"

\*\*\*

Clint Adams was drifting.

He had recently suffered the loss of his longtime friend, Rick Hartman. As a result, he was dealing with depression, and disinterest. These days he didn't want to get involved in anyone else's problems.

Years ago, when his friend Wild Bill Hickok was shot in the back and killed, he took refuge in a bottle of whiskey. This time, although Rick was also shot in the back, he resisted the urge to drink. After Hickok, it had taken him too long to climb out of the bottle. He didn't want to go through that, again.

So he was drifting from town to town, beer to beer, woman to woman, poker game to poker game, not making any new friends, just killing time and moving on.

In a small town in Kansas a little boy stepped out, pointed a wooden gun at him and said, "Stick 'em up. I'm the Tall Texan!"

"Good for you," Clint said and kept walking.

Another time, in a larger town in Missouri, he was eating a steak in a café, reached over and snagged a newspaper from the empty table next to him. The front page had a story about another robbery pulled by "The Tall Texan."

"He's makin' a real name fer himself, ain't he?" his waiter said.

"What's that?" Clint asked.

"That Tall Texan," the waiter said. "He's a legend now, ya know. They're writing books about him."

"Is that so?" Clint folded the newspaper and set it aside.

"Anythin' else, sir?" the waiter asked.

"No, thanks."

***

Heading back West, Clint found himself in Abilene in the Magnolia House Hotel. He was sitting in a wooden chair on the front porch, wondering where his drifting would find him next, when the desk clerk came out.

"Got a telegram for you, Mr. Adams."

"Telegram?" Clint said. "Who knows I'm here?"

"If you'd like to send a reply, I can do that for you, sir," the clerk said.

"I'll let you know."

He tipped the clerk and accepted the telegram. When he unfolded it, the first thing he saw was the name "Pinkerton." Clint and the Pinkertons had a checkered past, starting with working for Allan during the war, and then again later when he started his detective agency. They didn't get along real well, but respected each other. Then, after old Allan died, his boys William and Robert took over the agency, William in Chicago and Robert in

San Francisco. He had done work for each of them, at times when they had something that roused his interest.

This telegram was from Robert, the younger of the two brothers. Clint didn't like either one of them, and he liked Robert the least. But there was a name in the telegram that caught his eyes. It was "The Tall Texan."

He read the entire telegram. It said: HAVE YOU HEARD OF THE TALL TEXAN? IT TAKES A LEGEND TO CATCH A LEGEND. That was it.

Clint assumed the Pinkertons had been hired to catch this man. Robert was trying to flatter him with the "legend" talk.

Clint didn't flatter easily, but he had been hearing about this "Tall Texan" quite a bit, lately. Maybe it was time to stop drifting and moping and get something done.

He went inside to have the clerk send a reply.

# Chapter Two

Whenever he was in San Francisco Clint usually stayed at a casino in Portsmouth Square, the virtual center of town which was surrounded by gambling houses and saloons. This time he chose The Parker House, which was the first gambling establishment and hotel ever opened there. He wasn't really interested in the gambling aspect of the place, he just wanted to treat himself well and stay at one of the finest hotels in the city. Besides, he was going to get the Pinkertons to pay for it.

He had stopped in Las Vegas, New Mexico first to ask his friend John Locke to care for his Tobiano while he was away. He didn't see the point of taking the horse all the way there with him. Once that was done, he caught the train to San Francisco, arrived at the Parker House in need of a hot bath. The hotel had modern amenities, which included a bathtub in a water closet just off his room.

He decided to have that hot bath and then a thick steak, letting a meeting with Robert Pinkerton wait til the next day. So instead of going to the Pinkerton office, he sent word to Robert by hotel messenger that he was at the Parker House. He received word back that Pinkerton would meet him there for supper.

Although he wasn't in San Francisco for the gambling, he spent the day not only in the Parker House but the Exchange which was on one side and the El Dorado which was on the other.

Rather than get involved in a poker game, he threw money away in each place playing the roulette wheel and the wheel of fortune.

He had managed to lose a hundred dollars when the time came for him to meet Pinkerton in the dining room of the Parker House.

Clint made sure he arrived after Robert, wanting to make the younger Pinkerton wait. It was a game he played over the years with all the Pinkertons. Allan had tried several times to get Clint to join his agency, and the bone of contention between the two had always been Clint's refusal. Robert and William didn't try to recruit him, but they did, on occasion, draw him in with an interesting case.

Pinkerton, having eaten in restaurants with Clint before, had made sure to get a back table, from where they'd be able to see the entire room.

Clint spotted Pinkerton as soon as he entered and didn't wait for anyone to show him the way. As he approached the table, the dapper Robert stood. The two men shook hands and then sat.

"I hope you don't mind," Robert said, "but I ordered wine for both of us."

"That's fine," Clint said, although he would have preferred a cold beer.

He sat down across from Robert Pinkerton, noticed that the man had gained weight, and looked older. He didn't think he had yet turned forty.

"How did you find out where I was to send me a telegram?" Clint asked.

"I didn't," Robert said. "We sent that same telegram to about forty different places throughout the Southwest. I was hoping one of them would find you."

"And it did," Clint said. "How long did it take?"

"Weeks."

"And you still need me for the same job?"

"Oh, yes," Pinkerton said.

The waiter came with two glasses of red wine. Both men ordered a steak dinner.

"Okay, then, Robert," Clint said, "what's this about the Tall Texan?"

"You've heard of him?" Pinkerton asked.

"I've been hearing things about someone called the Tall Texan."

"What've you heard?"

"That he's a legend," Clint said. "That they write books about him."

"They write dime novels about you, too," Pinkerton pointed out. In fact, you've both been written up in *Cowboy Thrill Magazine*.

"I don't read those things," Clint said.

The waiter brought a bowl filled with grilled onions and set it down between their plates. Apparently, Pinkerton ate there often.

Robert took the bowl and dumped about half of it onto his steak, then held it out to Clint.

"Help yourself."

Clint took the other half and did the same.

"Thanks."

"This Tall Texan," Pinkerton said, cutting his steak, "is like Robin Hood. Do you know that legend?"

"I do," Clint said. "He stole from the rich and gave to the poor."

"It's said he never killed anyone, unless it was in self-defense against the Sheriff of Nottingham. The Tall Texan is the same. He robs trains and coaches, banks, and he never kills anyone. And he's still the most wanted man in the Southwest."

"And you're the sheriff of Nottingham?" Clint asked.

Pinkerton smiled.

"I suppose in this instance, I am."

"And who am I?" Clint asked. "In this little play?"

"You," Pinkerton said, "are the legend we'll send to catch the legend."

# Chapter Three

"Who's hired you to find him?" Clint asked.

"Let's just say we have a vested interest in putting his career to an end," Robert said.

"How many of your operatives have you sent after him?"

Robert Pinkerton hesitated, then said, "Six, five men and a woman."

"A woman?"

"It's an experiment," Pinkerton said. "Female operatives can come in handy, at times."

"What happened to the six?"

"Nothing," Pinkerton said. "They didn't get the job done. None of them were hurt."

"Has the government gotten involved?" Clint asked.

"They sent a few agents out to try to find him," Pinkerton said. "Artemus Gordon, Canyon O'Grady . . . neither got the job done, either."

"Jim West?"

"He's busy elsewhere."

"Have you tried Talbot Roper?"

Pinkerton tightened his jaw.

"Roper won't work for us," he said. "You know that."

"I just thought you might've asked."

"No," Pinkerton said.

"But you're asking me."

"Yes," Pinkerton said. "You've worked with us before."

"When the case piqued my interest."

"And this one doesn't?"

"Not yet," Clint said. "I'm not sure I want to go after a Robin Hood imposter. That could make me pretty unpopular."

"He's a thief," Pinkerton said. "Not a hero."

"Now you're using words like thief and hero," Clint said. "Before it was just 'legend.'"

"Maybe we should concentrate on our meals," Pinkerton said, "and just . . . chat."

"With all due respect," Clint said, "you and I have very little to chat about."

Pinkerton smiled grimly. "Let's give it a try."

\*\*\*

Clint turned out to be right. They had little to chat about. Clint asked about Robert's brother, William.

"I don't like to talk about my brother," Pinkerton said.

Pinkerton expressed his regrets about the murder of Rick Hartman.

"I don't want to talk about Rick Hartman," Clint said.

"Can't say I blame you for that."

They finished eating and the waiter cleared their plates.

"Anythin' else, gents?" the elderly waiter asked.

"Coffee," Pinkerton said.

"I'll have a cold beer," Clint said.

"Anythin' with those drinks?"

They both said no.

"Momentarily," the waiter said.

"Clint," Pinkerton said, "the Tall Texan can't keep this up forever."

"Meaning what?"

"Meaning eventually he's going to hurt somebody," Pinkerton said, "maybe even kill them. He needs to be stopped before that happens."

"Stopped how?"

"Arrested," Pinkerton said. "Put in prison."

"Not killed?"

"What makes you think I want you to kill him?" Pinkerton asked.

"I know you consider me a hired gun, Pinkerton," Clint said.

"I used to," Pinkerton admitted. "Not anymore. You've proven yourself more than once."

"Well, thanks for that," Clint said, "but I'd still like to give this some thought."

"That's up to you," Pinkerton said. "I hope your answer will be yes."

"Do you have any idea where he is now?" Clint asked. "Or where he's going to hit next?"

"Nobody ever knows his next move," Pinkerton said.

"Then what makes you think I'd be able to catch him?" Clint asked.

"You don't think like the rest of us, Clint," Pinkerton said. "Like I said, it takes a legend to catch a legend."

"You're saying I think like a legend?" Clint asked. "Or like a thief?"

"I'm saying you and he are different from others," Pinkerton said, "but you may also be somewhat alike."

"So I have to figure out where he's going to hit next and get there first."

"Something no one else has been able to do," Robert Pinkerton said.

Clint sipped his cold beer and admitted to himself that his interest had been piqued. But he was still going to make Pinkerton wait for an answer.

# Chapter Four

After supper Pinkerton left the Parker House, said he was going home.

"I'll be in my office on Market Street tomorrow," he told Clint. "You can give me your answer there."

"I'll see you in the morning then," Clint said.

Pinkerton left Clint standing in the Parker House lobby. Clint had three options: go to his room, go to the saloon or the casino. He decided against gambling, but felt he could use one more beer before going to his room.

In the saloon he paused to look around, saw that it was about three-quarters filled with men wearing expensive suits. They were either local businessmen, or gamblers taking a break from the casino.

He approached the bar and found space with no trouble.

"Sir?" the tuxedoed bartender said.

"A beer, please."

"Are you a guest of the hotel, sir?"

"Yes, I am," Clint said, showing the barkeep his key.

"What room, sir?"

"Two-fourteen," Clint said.

"Very good, sir," the bartender said. He drew a beer and set it down in front of Clint. "The cost of the drink will be added to your room bill, sir."

"Thank you."

Clint grabbed his beer and turned to drink it while he looked the place over. He had been there before, but it had been a while. Somehow, the saloon looked larger to him, now.

He turned back to the bar, leaned on it and nursed his beer while he thought about Robert Pinkerton's request. Clint tried not to pay attention to reputations, because he knew first-hand how exaggerated they could be. But he *had* been hearing the name Tall Texan quite a bit, lately. It might be time to push his mourning for Rick Hartman to the back of his mind and start living again.

He finished the beer and left the empty glass on the bar.

"Another?" the bartender asked.

"No, thanks," Clint said. "That'll do it for me to-night."

"Very well," the bartender said, taking the empty glass. "Good night, sir."

"Good night."

Clint went back to the lobby, resisted the siren sound of the chips in the casino, and went to his room. Once there, he hung his gunbelt on the bedpost, as usual, removed his boots and settled onto the large, firm mattress bed to read for a while before turning in. He kind of wished he'd had a copy of Robin Hood . . .

\*\*\*

When the knock came on his door, it roused him. He was almost asleep with the Dickens collection he'd been reading laying heavy on his chest.

He set the book aside, swung his feet to the floor, and removed the gun from the hanging holster.

"Who is it?"

"Mr. Adams?" a woman's voice called out. "You don't know me, but I need to speak with you."

Clint opened the door a crack, saw an attractive brunette standing in the hall alone.

"What's this about?" he asked.

"The Pinkertons," she said. "I know you ate with Robert Pinkerton tonight. I need to speak with you about that."

He opened the door wider, looked both ways in the hall, then back at her.

"It's late," he said. "If you don't mind coming into a man's room—"

Before he could finish, she eased past him into his room. He shrugged and closed the door.

16

"You won't need that gun," she said, spreading her arms. "I'm unarmed."

She was carrying a drawstring purse; he could see there was nothing as heavy as a gun in it. He walked to the bedpost and holstered his gun. His shirt was open and his feet were bare, but none of that seemed to bother the woman, who was wearing a dress that buttoned up to her neck and hung to her ankles.

"You have me at a disadvantage," he said. "You know my name—"

"I'm Matty Cole," she said. "My name's actually Mathilda, but I hate it, so everybody calls me Matty."

"Why not Tilly?" he asked.

She made a face.

"I hate that even more."

"Well then, Matty," he said, folding his arms, "what's on your mind?"

"I know Robert Pinkerton is trying to hire you to track down a man called the Tall Texan."

"And how do you know that?" he asked.

"He flooded the Southwest with telegrams trying to get your attention," she said. "Word gets around."

"And why does that matter to you?" he asked. "Wait. Are you one of the lady Pinkertons Robert was telling me about?"

"No, sir," she said, "I'm not a detective. I'm a journalist."

"Ah."

"I'd like to write the story about you and the Tall Texan."

# Chapter Five

"You should have told me that from the start," Clint said.

"Why is that?" she asked.

"Because then I wouldn't have let you in." He walked to the door and opened it. "Have a nice night."

"That's it?" she asked. "You don't want to know why I'm here?"

"You're here for a story," he said. "I don't have one to give you."

She stood firm.

"The Gunsmith going after the Tall Texan," she said, "that's a story."

"First of all, I haven't decided that I'm going after him," he said, "and second, if, and when I do, there's no story in it for you. At least, not from me. Try talking to the Pinkertons. They like the publicity."

"Mr. Adams," she said, walking right up to him, "the public has a right to know."

"No," he said, "they don't, Miss Cole."

"Matty, please."

"Good night, Miss Cole," he said.

"Good night, Mr. Adams."

She went out into the hall, and he closed the door behind her. Instead of going back to Dickens, he went to bed.

***

In the morning he had a leisurely breakfast in the Parker House dining room, choosing to let Pinkerton wait a little longer for his decision.

After that he presented himself at the Pinkerton office on Market Street. It was on the fourth floor and even though there was an elevator, Clint preferred to use the stairs.

"Do you have an appointment?" the attractive woman at the reception desk asked.

"Let's say I'm expected," he replied.

"Your name?"

"Clint Adams."

"Please wait here."

She stood up, went through the door behind her, returned moments later with another woman. This one was older and better dressed, with a stern countenance that had caused lines to crease her face over the years.

"Mr. Adams," she said, "my name is Mrs. Lake. I'm Mr. Pinkerton's assistant."

"It's nice to meet you."

"Please follow me."

They went back through the same door with her leading him down a long hall. He had been there before, but Pinkerton had apparently changed offices.

They reached a closed door. She opened it and stepped aside.

"You may go in."

"Thank you, Mrs. Lake."

He entered. Robert Pinkerton was seated at a huge, oak desk in front of a large window. He stood as Clint approached his desk. They shook hands.

"Thanks for coming," he said. "Have a seat."

They sat across from each other.

"Have you come to a decision?"

"That depends."

"On what?"

"Do you know a woman named Matty Cole?"

Pinkerton frowned.

"I don't believe so."

"She says she's a journalist," Clint said. "She came to my room last night to talk about the Tall Texan."

"What did she want to know?"

"She wanted a story," Clint said.

"What did you tell her?"

"I kicked her out," Clint said.

"Did she say how she found out about you being here?" he asked.

"She said it was because you sent out so many telegrams," Clint explained, "blanketing almost the entire Southwest with them."

"But how did she know we had met?" Pinkerton asked. "And where you were staying?"

"She has her sources," Clint said.

"Well," Pinkerton said, "I can assure you her source didn't come from here."

Clint studied the man, and decided he was telling the truth.

"All right, then," he said.

"So have you decided?"

Clint made the man wait a couple of beats before answering.

"Yes," Clint said. "I'm going to do what I can to find your man and bring him in."

Pinkerton took a deep breath and let it out.

"That's good to hear," he said. "Do you know where you intend to start?"

"I haven't got a clue," Clint replied.

# Chapter Six

"Where was the Tall Texan's first robbery?" Clint asked.

"A small east Texas town near Nacogdoches, called Woodriver."

"What was it he robbed?"

"A bank."

"How long ago was that?"

Pinkerton thought a moment.

"It must have been about four years."

"Why there?"

"What?"

"Did you ever ask yourself why he hit a bank in a small town like that?" Clint asked.

"There have been so many other robberies—"

"How much did he get from that one?" Clint asked.

"I don't know," Pinkerton said. "It was a small town, a small bank. It couldn't have been a lot."

"How many other jobs did he pull in Texas?"

Pinkerton opened a folder on his desk.

"Seven."

"In which part of Texas?"

Pinkerton looked at the file again.

"All in East Texas."

"And his other jobs?"

"They've been scattered throughout Louisiana, Arkansas, Oklahoma Territories, and Kansas."

"The others who have hunted for him—lawmen, bounty hunters, government agents, your people—where have they looked?"

"From what I know," Pinkerton said, "they go to wherever he pulled his last job."

"And in this case, where would that be?"

"It was a bank in Wichita."

Clint stood up and walked to the window, so he could look down at San Francisco.

"Tell me something," he said. "Does he always work alone?"

"From all the eyewitness accounts that have been compiled," Pinkerton said, "he's been alone ever since then."

"He's been alone when pulling the job," Clint said. "That doesn't mean he didn't have somebody working with him while planning it."

"That's true."

Clint turned and looked at Pinkerton.

"I think part of the problem has been starting a search for him in the last place he pulled a job."

"So where would you start?" Pinkerton asked.

"The first place."

"Why go back four years," Pinkerton asked, "when there's a fresh place to start?"

"Because I'm still curious why Woodriver would be his first," Clint said.

"Do you have a theory, already?"

"Yes," Clint said. "I'm thinking his first job was a test run, and he pulled it close to home."

Pinkerton frowned.

"Nobody's come up with that theory before," he said. "I wonder why?"

"It's logical to go to the site of the most recent job," Clint said. "And I'm thinking that so far, everyone involved has been logical."

"So you're going to take the opposite tact."

"I don't want to just repeat everyone's mistakes," Clint said. "I've got to do something different."

"And that's why I said you're different from the rest of us," Pinkerton said.

"Who's the last one of your operatives to work on this?" Clint asked.

"The woman," Pinkerton said. "Her name is Abigail West."

"I don't know her," Clint said. He knew she was no relation to his friend, Jim, who had no sisters.

"No," Pinkerton said, "she was hired only last year."

"I'd like to talk to her before I leave for Texas," Clint said.

"How about tonight at the Parker House?" Pinkerton said. "We can all have supper."

"Agreed," Clint said, "except I'd like it to be just her and me."

Pinkerton frowned.

"Why?"

"I want her to speak freely," Clint said. "She won't do that with her boss there."

"You're probably right."

"Are you sleeping with her?" Clint asked.

"What?" Pinkerton seemed taken aback by the question. "No! Why the hell would you ask me that?"

"I just want to make sure she's going to talk straight with me," Clint said.

"She'll tell you everything she knows," Pinkerton said. "I can promise you that."

"I'll need you to take care of my hotel," Clint said, "and I'll need expense money."

"I'll have it dropped off at your hotel," Pinkerton promised.

"Then if that happens tonight," Clint said, "I'll catch a train tomorrow morning."

"It'll be there tonight," Pinkerton said. "Would you like me to have Abby bring it?"

"No," Clint said, "let's keep my meeting with Abby separate."

"Very well."

Clint headed for the door, then stopped.

"Were any jobs pulled in New Mexico?"

Pinkerton referred to the folder.

"No, none."

"When the money is delivered," Clint said, "have it accompanied by a copy of that file, will you?"

"Done," Pinkerton said. "And will you keep in touch?"

"You'll hear from me the minute I know something," Clint said. "Not before."

"I suppose that's fair." Pinkerton started to stand.

"If you wait, I can have my assistant show you out."

"No need," Clint said. "I know the way."

He left the office, walked down the hall to the reception area, where the attractive girl smiled at him.

"What's your name?" he asked.

"Nancy."

"Nancy, do you know Abigail West?"

"Oh, yes sir," she said. "I know Abby."

"What can you tell me about her?"

"Well," Nancy said, "right now, she's the only female operative in the Pinkertons. There've been others, but they haven't lasted. Abby's different."

"How so?"

"She's smart, brave, loyal . . . and oh, she's funny."

"I see," he said. "Well, thanks a lot."

"Any time, sir," she said with a smile. "Call on me . . . anytime."

# Chapter Seven

The file and expense money showed up at the front desk of the Palace House before Abigail West did. It gave Clint time to sit in his room and go through the file. The names of all the places the Tall Texan had robbed, and all the eyewitnesses were in the file. But it would take him too long to go to each place and talk to each person. He'd need help to do that. Maybe his friend Talbot Roper, the best private detective he knew, would help him, even though Roper didn't want to work for the Pinkertons.

But before that, he was going to follow up on his theory about Woodriver.

When he finished going through the file, he closed it and went down to the lobby. There was a woman waiting there impatiently with folded arms.

"Are you Clint Adams?" she asked, as he approached.

"I am. You're Abigail West?"

"You've kept me waiting," she said.

"Sorry about that," he said. "I'll make it up to you by treating you to dinner."

"It better be a good one."

"I guess that'll be up to you," Clint said. "Come on."

He walked into the dining room and to a back table.

"Why don't we sit in front?" she asked. "There are empty tables."

"I prefer to sit where I can see the whole room," he said.

"Ah, yes," she said, "your reputation. You're always on the lookout for somebody taking a shot at you, aren't you?"

"I'm afraid I am," he said.

They sat across from each other at the table. He studied her for a moment. She looked to be in her late twenties, a solidly built, attractive girl with ash blonde hair worn tied in back.

When the waiter came, before he could even speak, Abby West told the man firmly, "Bring me the most expensive meal on the menu."

"Yes, Ma'am,"

Clint ordered steak.

"Mr. Pinkerton said I had to meet you for dinner," she said. "Or I wouldn't be here."

"Is that why you have such an attitude?" he asked.

"You wanna know why I have an attitude?" she asked. "Pinkerton took me off the Tall Texan case. He says I have to help you with it now." She stuck her chin out. "I could've caught him all by myself."

"Look," Clint said, "I had nothing to do with you being taken off the case. That's between you and Pinkerton. As far as I know, nobody's on it now. That's why Robert asked me to look into it."

"Well then, be my guest," she said. "Look into it. Why am I here?"

"You were the last one to work on the case," he said. "I just thought you might have something to tell me."

"Oh, I have something to tell you," she said, "and to tell Robert Pinkerton."

"If you don't like working for Robert, why don't you quit?" he asked.

"You'd like that, wouldn't you?" she asked. "Well, I'm not quitting, and I'm not going to stop looking for the Tall Texan. Whataya think of that?"

"That's up to you," Clint said. "I guess that means you won't do anything to help me."

"Not a damn thing," she said.

"Well then," he said, "I guess we should just eat. Hope you enjoy your lobster."

"Oh, believe me," she said. "I intend to."

# Chapter Eight

Abby West pushed her plate away and wiped her mouth with a cloth napkin. Her meal must have been good, because she seemed more agreeable, now.

"All right," she said. "What do you want to know?"

He put his knife and fork down.

"Just whatever you know," he said.

"He's tall," she said, "and he's from Texas."

Clint stared at her.

"Oh, all right!" she spat. "Every witness I spoke to said that he was polite and soft-spoken."

"And what does he look like?"

"He usually wears a bandana across the bottom of his face," she said. "A couple of women told me that he had kind eyes."

"What about weapons?"

"A pistol," she said. "Nobody knows what kind."

"And he's never shot anyone?"

"As far as I could find out," she said, "he's never even cocked the hammer back."

"Tell me," Clint said, "did the people he rob feel threatened?"

She hesitated a moment.

"No, I don't think so," she finally said.

"What were the jobs you investigated?" he asked.

"A train that stopped in Wichita after he robbed it," she said. "And a bank in Wichita."

"Two jobs in the same town?"

"He robbed the train well outside of Wichita," she said. "The bank was in Wichita."

"He held up the train alone?" Clint asked.

"Yes."

"That's usually a job for more than one man," Clint said. "One man trying to rob a train, so much can go wrong."

"But the victims all cooperated," she said.

"Was the car full?"

"No," she said, "about half full."

"What about the bank in Wichita?"

"Several employees, a few customers, and the bank manager," she said.

"And nobody tried to stop him?"

"No."

"And nobody resisted?"

"Not that I know of."

"So he's a nice man, he asks for their money and valuables, and they give them to him," Clint said.

"Seems so," she said.

"But he does have a gun."

"Oh, yes," she said, "he always has a gun."

"Well," he said, taking his napkin from his lap and laying it on the table, "thanks for talking with me, Miss West."

"Abby," she said. "You should call me Abby if we're going to work together."

He looked surprised.

"Who says we're going to work together?"

"I figure if you're working on this case," she said, "and I continue to work on it, then we'll be working against each other. That doesn't make sense to me."

"What's your boss going to say when he hears you're still working on it?" Clint asked.

She pressed her forefinger to her lovely lips. Her attitude had changed over dinner softening her face.

"What do you say we don't tell him?" she asked. "I'll just come along with you to Wichita."

"I'm not going to Wichita," he said.

"But . . . that's where the last job happened," she said. "Where are you going?"

"Woodriver," he said.

"Texas?" she asked. "But that . . . that was the first job . . ."

"I know."

"Why go there?"

"Because everyone else—you included—has already tried investigating from the most recent job."

"So you think starting at the beginning—"

"You can't come, Abby," he said.

"Why not?"

"I don't need you," he said. "You've told me everything you know."

She smiled. "Have I?"

\*\*\*

They left the dining room and Clint walked her to the front door.

"You're going to get yourself in trouble, Abby," he said. "Pinkerton might fire you."

"Not if I find the Tall Texan he won't," she said.

"And working this alone could be dangerous."

"If you're worried about me," she said, "then let me work with you."

"Abby," he said, then paused before he said, "I'll think about it."

35

# Chapter Nine

In the morning Clint checked out and caught a horse drawn cab, in front of the hotel, to the train station. Before riding to Woodriver, Texas he was going back to Las Vegas, New Mexico and pick up his Tobiano from John Locke's ranch. If he was going to find the Tall Texan, he needed an animal beneath him that he could trust.

Riding the train, he looked around the crowded car, wondering if he'd be able to stand up, draw his gun and rob everyone without someone trying to stop him? What was it this Tall Texan had that made people give in without a fight? Good manners? A big gun? A combination of both? And what about Abby West? Was she going to get in the way? She'd be pretty mad when she discovered he'd left San Francisco without seeing her again.

When he got to John Locke's ranch in Las Vegas, he spent one night, having supper with Locke in town.

"I've heard of this fella," Locke said, over steaks. "Seems to have made quite a name for himself."

"Have you ever thought about going after him?" Clint asked.

"Can't say I have," Locke said. "He hasn't killed anyone, has he?"

"No," Clint said, and then added, "not yet."

"What do you mean?" Locke asked. "You expect him to?"

"How many armed robberies can you pull before you finally hurt someone?" Clint asked.

"Well," Locke said, "if he kills someone, the price on his head would go up. So unless you stop him before he does that, maybe I will go after him."

"Why don't you come with me now?" Clint asked. "The price on his head is decent."

"I've got two others I'm lookin' for right now," Locke said. "If you still need me when I'm done, I'll give you a hand."

"Fair enough," Clint said.

They went back to the ranch, where Clint slept in the bunkhouse because Locke's house had only one bedroom. In the morning, Clint saddled the Tobiano and walked him out of the barn.

"I'll be headin' out this afternoon," Locke said.

"Where to?" Clint asked.

"North," Locke said. "I'm afraid I'll be spendin' some time in the Dakotas."

"Make sure you dress warm then," Clint said.

"Good luck finding this Tall Texan," Locke said. "Let me know if he ever kills anyone, huh?"

"Sometimes," Clint said, "you're kind of a sonofabitch, aren't you, John?"

"I specialize in catchin' killers, Clint," Locke said. "So sue me."

"If it comes to that," Clint said, "if he does kill someone, I'll let you know."

The two men shook hands. Clint mounted up and rode away.

***

Clint found the town of Woodriver small and quiet, but not at all unpleasant. People smiled at him as he rode down the street, men and women both. When he saw the bank, he reined the Tobiano in and went inside.

There was one teller behind a barred window, and one woman seated at a desk.

"Can I help you, sir?" the teller asked, flashing a welcoming smile.

"I'd like to talk to the bank manager."

"May I tell him what it's about?"

"A robbery that happened here four years ago," Clint said. "Did you work here then?"

"Oh, no, I didn't," the clerk said.

"And the current manager? Was he here?"

"Mr. Cooke," the teller said, "yes, he was."

Clint looked over at the woman at the desk.

"And the lady? Was she here?"

"No," the teller said, "she and I were hired around the same time last year."

"All right, then," Clint said. "Can I see Mr. Cooke?"

"Just a minute," the teller said. "Can I tell him your name?"

"Clint Adams."

"Oh my . . . just a minute."

The teller went to the door of the manager's office, knocked and entered. When he reappeared, an older man was with him, looking agitated.

"Mr. Adams?" the manager said. "The Gunsmith? Have you found our money?"

"Are you Mr. Cooke, the manager?"

"I'm Henry Cooke."

"I'm sorry," Clint said, "I don't have your money, but I'd like to talk to you about the robbery."

"Of course, of course," Cooke said. "Come with me to my office."

Clint thanked the teller, then followed Cooke into his office.

# Chapter Ten

"What brings you here four years after the fact?" Cooke asked, once he had seated himself behind his desk.

Clint sat across from him.

"I've been asked to try and track this thief down," Clint said. "Instead of starting at his most recent robbery, I thought I'd start with his first."

"I'm afraid I can't tell you much," Cooke said. "He walked in, brandished a weapon and asked for the money. We gave it to him."

"He *asked* for the money?"

"That's right."

"He didn't *demand* it?"

Cooke looked surprised.

"Now that you mention it, no," he said. "He simply . . . asked."

"And you just . . . gave it to him."

"Well . . . he did have a gun," Cooke pointed out.

"So you were in fear for your life?" Clint asked.

"I . . . I suppose so."

"You either were, or you weren't, Mr. Cooke," Clint said. "Were you afraid he'd shoot you?"

"It . . . it never got that far," Cooke said.

"What about the other people in the bank?"

"My clerk and teller both quit after that," Cooke said.

"So they were afraid?"

"Not exactly," Cooke said. "They quit when they got married and left town."

"So it had nothing to do with the robbery?"

"I don't believe so."

"According to the facts I've been given," Clint said, "there were customers in the bank."

"That's right," Cooke said. "Two."

"Do they still live in town?"

"They do," Cooke said. "They each have a business."

"Can you give me their names, please?"

Cooke wrote the names down and spoke them while doing so.

"Orlin Brown owns the general store, and Stanley Trotman manages the Tributary Hotel."

He handed Clint the slip of paper.

"Thank you," Clint said. "What about the sheriff? Is he the same lawman who was here then?"

"Oh yes," Cooke said. "Grant Mayhew has been the sheriff here for many years. You'll find his office right down the street."

"I assume he went looking for the thief?"

Clint nodded. "He looked. Not for very long, but he looked."

"I understand the thief was very tall," Clint said.

"Indeed," Cooke said. "That's why they call him the Tall Texan."

"Are there—or were there—any men living around here who were that tall?"

"As tall as he was?" Cooke said. "No."

"Well," Clint said, standing, "thanks for talking to me, Mr. Cooke."

"Mr. Adams," Cooke said, "do you think you might, ah, get our money back?"

"After four years?" Clint said. "Even if I manage to track him down and bring him in, I doubt it. How much are we talking about?"

"Almost four thousand dollars."

"That's all he got?" Clint asked.

"Well," Cooke said, "we had just opened."

"He robbed the bank first thing in the morning?" Clint asked.

"No, no," Cooke said, "I mean, we had just opened for business. We were a new bank."

"Oh, I see. I'm much obliged for your time, Mr. Cooke."

As Clint left the man's office, Cooke was sitting slumped behind his desk. The four thousand dollars must have been weighing heavily on his mind. But in the long run, it really wasn't very much, considering some of the other jobs The Tall Texan had pulled. Clint was more convinced than ever that the Woodriver job had been a practice run for the thief.

After leaving the bank, Clint decided to board his horse and get a hotel room before he continued. He found a small livery at the end of the main street, told the hostler he didn't know how many days he was going to be there.

"Fine lookin' horse," the old man said. "I'm gonna treat 'im good."

"Thanks."

He went to the Tributary Hotel and got himself a room with no trouble. There wasn't much in this small town to bring people in. The room was small, sparsely furnished, and dusty.

Clint left his saddlebags and rifle on the bed and went back downstairs.

He stepped outside the hotel, hesitating there to study the street. It was midday and there was very little activity. If it wasn't for the fact that he had already been in the bank, livery stable, and hotel, he might have thought it was a ghost town.

He stepped into the street and headed for the sheriff's office.

# Chapter Eleven

When he entered the sheriff's office, he saw that the man's desk was against a wall, putting his back to the door. He found that odd.

The man at the desk heard the door open and turned. He looked to be in his fifties, and when he stood, Clint saw he was wearing a well-worn gunbelt and a somewhat dented and tarnished sheriff's badge on his chest.

"'afternoon," the lawman said. "Can I help ya with somethin'?"

"Sheriff," Clint said, "my name's Clint Adams."

"Well," the man said, "the Gunsmith." He was old enough not to be impressed with Clint, as a younger man might have been. He had probably met plenty of men over the years who some people called legends. "What brings you to Woodriver?"

"The Tall Texan, I'm afraid."

"Ah," the sheriff said, "our local hero."

"Is that what he's considered here?" Clint asked. "Even after robbing your bank. A local hero?"

"Well, not right away," the lawman said. "For a while he was just considered another thief. But when he started makin' a name for himself, folks started changin' their minds." The man stuck out his hand. "Mayhew's my name." They shook hands. "Why don't you sit and tell me what's on your mind?"

They both sat.

"I've got a bottle of whiskey in my desk, if you're interested."

"I guess a small one would be okay, until I can get to the saloon for a beer. I just rode in."

The sheriff took a bottle of whiskey and two coffee cups from his bottom drawer. He poured two fingers into each mug and handed one to Clint.

"Thanks."

"You huntin' bounty now?" Sheriff Mayhew asked.

"Not exactly," Clint said. "I've been asked by the Pinkertons to try and track this fella down. Seems nobody else has been able to do it—lawmen, bounty hunters, government agents, the military—"

"—and the Pinkerton Agency, huh?" Mayhew said.

"That's right."

"Excuse me for askin'," the lawman said, "but what makes them think you'll be able to do it?"

"Pinkerton has this crazy idea that it takes a legend to catch a legend," Clint said.

"That's funny," Mayhew said. "I mean, you've been you for a lot longer than this Tall Texan's been around. The idea that you're both equal legends is silly."

45

"Well, I think the word legend is silly, no matter how long somebody's been around," Clint said. "I'm just a man."

"With a reputation."

"With a past," Clint said. "In any case, I've decided to start my search here."

"I heard the most recent robbery was in Wichita," Mayhew said. "Why not start there?"

"That's the logical first step," Clint said, "but so far, logic hasn't been successful. So I'm going a different way."

"Startin' here?" Mayhew asked. "That fella hasn't been seen here since the robbery four years ago."

"How do you know that?"

"What?"

"How do you know he isn't here?" Clint asked. "Nobody's ever seen his face. He could be right across the street."

"That might be true," Mayhew said, "but . . . come on, why would he still be here?"

"Maybe because he lives here," Clint said. "He pulls his jobs, then comes back home."

"If this is his home," Mayhew said, "why would he have robbed our bank."

"For practice," Clint said. "His first job. Maybe just to be sure he could do it."

"I'm curious," the sheriff said. "How do you intend to find him?"

"I'm not sure, yet," Clint said. "I thought a good first step would be talking with you. All I have to work with is the man's height."

"Ah, yes," Mayhew said, "the name, 'Tall Texan.' He's supposed to be . . . what? Six-and-a-half feet tall?"

"I don't know," Clint said. "You'd know that better than I would. I assume you questioned everyone who was in the bank that day."

"Oh, I spoke to them," Mayhew said. "I talked to five people and got five different descriptions."

"They must've all agreed on something," Clint said.

"Oh, they did," the lawman said. "While they all said he was polite, and tall, the guesses I got ran from six-foot-four to six-foot-eight."

"And build?"

"I got slim, thin, solid, strong . . . the lady clerk said she was sure he was handsome."

"I wonder how she could tell that?" Clint said. "I've heard he covers his face."

"Yes," Mayhew said, "it was just a feeling she had."

"Was that the woman who worked in the bank? The one who left to get married?"

"Yes," the sheriff said, "she left town."

"Too bad." Clint put the cup down. "Thanks for the drink."

"Any time," Mayhew said. "I assume you'll be here a while. Later we can have a beer in the saloon."

"I'll look forward to it," Clint said, and left the office.

# Chapter Twelve

It didn't take Clint long to walk from one end of town to the other. He found one saloon, but also a sign in the window of the general store that said it served drinks. He decided to go in there, since that's where he would find Orlin Brown.

The store was well stocked, the walls covered with shelves, and the shelves loaded with supplies. In the back of the store were two counters. Behind one was a collection of bottles, so Clint assumed the other was where you bought supplies. There was a white-haired man in his sixties standing there.

"Can I help ya, sir?" the man asked. "We've got everythin' you could need."

"Including a cold beer?" Clint asked.

"Step this way," the man said, indicating the second counter. He walked over and took up position behind it, drew Clint a beer from a single tap and set it on the wooden counter that acted as a bar.

"Thanks," Clint said. "I just rode in and need to wash away the trail dust." He drank down half the mug. The beer was not as cold as it might have been, but it did the trick.

"You'll find colder beer at the saloon down the street," the man admitted.

"It's fine," Clint said. "Are you Mr. Brown?"

"Orlin Brown," the man said, "at your service. And who are you?"

"Mr. Brown, my name's Clint Adams. I'd like to talk to you about the bank robbery four years ago."

The man looked surprised.

"Why's the Gunsmith interested in a penny ante bank robbery?" he asked.

"Penny ante?"

"Well," Brown said, "he didn't get much."

"I talked with Mr. Cooke over at the bank," Clint said. "He seems to still be pretty upset."

Brown laughed.

"Cooke squeezes every dime til it screams, Mister Adams," he said. "I don't wanna say he's cheap, but . . . well, he's cheap."

"So the town's not as upset as he is about the robbery?" Clint asked.

"I'm sure he told you the bank had just opened," Brown said. "Nobody lost their life savings. I think the Tall Texan knew that when he robbed it."

"Then why do you think he did it?"

"Truthfully?" Brown said. "I think he was testing himself. As it stands, he's gone on to do great things."

"Is that what you call robbing trains and coaches and banks?" Clint asked. "Great things?"

"He's become a legend, ain't he? You should know all about that kind of thing."

"I don't consider my past to be filled with great accomplishments, Mr. Brown," Clint said.

Brown grabbed Clint's mug and topped it off.

"Why are you here, Sir?" he asked, setting the mug in front of him.

"I'm trying to catch the thief," Clint said.

"And what makes you think you'll find him here?"

"I'm like you, Mr. Brown," Clint said. "I believe the first job was just a test. And I think perhaps he lived around here back then. Maybe he still does."

"All the stories say he wears a mask," Brown said.

"You were in the bank that day," Clint said. "What did he have on his face?"

"A bandana," Brown said, "covering the lower half."

"So you were able to see his eyes?"

"Oh, yes."

"And what did they tell you?"

"Well . . . probably that he was a young man," Brown said. "No lines or bags, like I have." He indicated his own face.

"I spoke with Sheriff Mayhew," Clint said. "He said one witness called him handsome."

"That was just the foolish woman who worked there," Brown said. "She got a romantic notion about him. There was no way to tell what he looked like."

"What did he sound like?"

"His voice was muffled."

"But surely you could tell if it was high, or low?"

"Just sort of . . . medium," Brown said.

"And his height?"

"Pretty tall," Brown said, "but he was wearing high boot heels."

"How tall are you, sir?" Clint asked.

"I'm six feet," Orlin Brown said, "but he towered above me."

"Was he already masked when he walked in?" Clint asked.

"That's a good question," Brown said. "I think he must've tugged it up over his face as he entered, so nobody outside would see a masked man entering the bank, but no one inside would see him without it."

"So he's tall, polite," Clint said, "and smart."

Brown smiled and said, "Looks that way."

"Did you lose any money that day, Mr. Brown?"

The storekeeper shook his head.

"I hadn't made a deposit yet," he said. "And he didn't take my money from my hand. He only took it from the bank."

"I see."

"Folks around here kinda like that we were the first ones he robbed," Orlin Brown said. "But I can't say any of us ever thought that he might live here. That's kinda excitin'."

"Maybe you'd like to spread that around, then? Clint said. "Let other people know the Tall Texan might live here, and that I'm looking for him."

"I might just do that," Brown said. "I'm always lookin' for somethin' to talk to folks about." He shook his head. "The Gunsmith and the Tall Texan. That really is somethin'!"

# Chapter Thirteen

Clint left the general store and walked over to the saloon. He thought about going to see Stanley Trotman at the hotel but decided to leave that until he was actually ready to return to his room.

The Victory Saloon was the only saloon in town, but in a place as small as Woodriver it wasn't busy. He didn't see that until he opened the door and entered. There were no batwings, just a regular door that was half opaque glass. There was plenty of room at tables, and at the bar.

Clint went to the bar and was greeted by a friendly, thirty-something bartender.

"Welcome to the Victory," he said. "What can I getcha?"

"A beer," Clint said. "A cold one."

"Only kind we got," the bartender said. "You gotta go to the general store for the warm ones."

"I know, I had one there already." Clint picked up the beer and sipped it. "Ah, that's what I wanted."

"What brings you to our town, friend?" the bartender asked. "Ain't much goin' on here."

"I heard this was the first place the Tall Texan ever robbed a bank."

"That's true." The bartender leaned on the bar.

"Were you here then?"

"Oh yeah," the man said, "I been the bartender here for over six years."

"You ever heard anyone in here talk about him?" Clint asked.

"Sure," the bartender said, "people in a saloon talk about everythin'."

"Ever hear anyone say they knew him?"

"Naw, nothin' like that," the man said. "Say, what's your interest, anyway?"

"Just curious," Clint said. "As to what I'm doing here, I'm passing through."

"On your way to where?"

"Nowhere in particular," Clint said. "I'm just drifting."

"We don't get a lot of drifters here," the bartender said. "What's your name?"

"Clint. What's yours?"

"Garrett," the bartender said.

Clint finished his beer and said, "Thanks for the drink." He dropped a coin on the bar and left. It probably wouldn't be long before the bartender heard he was in town and figured out who he had been talking to.

***

Clint went to his hotel and stopped at the front desk.

"Can I help you, Mr. Adams?" the young clerk asked.

"Yes, I was wondering if your manager was around?"

"Mr. Trotman?" the clerk asked. "Do you have a complaint?"

"No, nothing like that" Clint said. "I just want to talk to him."

"Well . . . he's in his office. I'll tell him you'd like to see him."

"Thank you."

The clerk left the desk, walked to a door in the back wall. He knocked and entered. He came out moments later and waved at Clint.

"You can go in, Mr. Adams," he said.

"Thank you."

Clint entered the office, found a man sitting behind a small, wooden desk. He was well-dressed, with hair and a beard that both looked recently trimmed.

"Clint Adams?" He stood. "I'm Stanley Trotman." They shook hands. "Please, have a seat. How can I help you?"

Clint sat and said, "I understand you were in the bank four years ago when it was held up."

Trotman frowned.

"You're interested in a four-year old bank robbery?" the hotel manager asked. "Why?"

"I'm interested in the Tall Texan."

"Ah, I see," Trotman said. "Well, yes, I was there."

"Can you tell me anything about him?" Clint asked.

"Probably just what everyone else has told you," Trotman said. "He robbed the bank at gunpoint."

"But he didn't take any money from you?"

"No."

"Did you lose any money in the robbery?"

"No," Trotman said, "I hadn't yet made a deposit for the hotel."

"So nobody seems upset about the bank robbery in this town," Clint said, "except for the manager."

"Cooke," Trotman said, with a laugh. "He's very cheap. If it had been a nickel rather than thousands, he'd still be upset."

"So there's nothing you can add to the description?" Clint asked. "Tall and pleasant?"

"That about sums it up," Trotman said. "Sorry I can't help."

"That's okay," Clint said, standing. "That's the same reaction I'm getting from everybody around here. Thanks for your time."

## Chapter Fourteen

Clint went to his room and sat on the bed. The Tall Texan's image seemed to be alive and well in Woodriver. Clint thought if he was actually six-and-a-half feet tall, or more, he wouldn't be able to hide if he actually lived in town. If he lived on the outskirts, he'd have to come in sooner or later for supplies.

It was Clint's experience that witnesses usually exaggerated what they saw. He figured the man was tall, but not as tall as folks were saying. The thief was probably over six feet, had no outstanding features, like big ears or a big nose. But what everybody was agreeing on that might be true was his manner. He was a gentleman thief, inviting people to give up their valuables, rather than demanding them.

If he lived in or around town, somebody was going to know it. He just had to find out who that somebody was. Maybe it was a woman. He was going to wait a few hours, and when it started to get dark go back to the saloon, have a beer or two, and sit and listen.

Until then, it was time to go back to Charles Dickens.

\*\*\*

The saloon wasn't lively, but it was busy. They had no music, no table games, no private poker games. There were two girls working the floor.

"Back again," Garrett, the bartender, said. "Another beer?"

"Yep. Can you have one of the girls bring it over to me at a table?"

"Sure."

Clint walked to an empty table against a wall and sat. There were men at nearby tables, and he could hear their conversations. A few of the men cast curious glances in his direction, but then looked away. He assumed in a town this size the word had gone out about who he was and why he was there.

"Here's your beer, Sir," a girl said, setting it down. She was pretty, with black hair and very pale, smooth skin.

"Can you sit for a minute?" he asked her.

"Um, not without a drink."

"What's your name?"

"Lori."

"Well, Lori you sit and I'll go to the bar and get you a drink. How's that?"

She giggled and said, "Suits me. Champagne."

"Of course."

He went to the bar and told Garrett, "Champagne for the lady."

"Comin' up." the bartender said.

He poured a glass and put it down in front of Clint.

"What do you think you'll find out from her?" he asked.

"I won't know that until I ask her, will I?" Clint said, picking up the champagne.

He carried the glass back to his table, set it down and sat across from her. He studied the girl for a moment while she sipped her drink. He put her at twenty-five or so.

"I don't suppose you were working here four years ago, were you?" he asked.

"No, sir," she said, "I only started two years ago."

"I see."

"But I've lived here all my life," she added.

"Well, that's good," Clint said. "Then you were around when the bank was robbed?"

"Oh yes, I was here," she said. "I lived in a house just outside of town with my Pa."

"And do you still live there?"

"No," she said. "Pa died, and I moved to town. I live with my Aunt."

"Does she approve of you working here?" Clint asked.

"To Aunt Kate, a job's a job," she said, with a shrug.

"So tell me," Clint said, "what do you know about the bank robbery?"

"I know the fella they say robbed it is called The Tall Texan," she said. "Well, he wasn't called that back then, but he is now."

"What was he called back then?"

She shrugged.

"I dunno," she said. "Nobody knows who he was. He just robbed the bank and rode out of town."

"Come on," he said, "somebody in this town must have an idea who he was."

"If they do," she said, "I never heard anybody say."

"I heard he was a tall man," Clint said.

"Well, I guess that's why they call 'im the Tall Texan," she said, with a laugh.

"You must've seen some tall men in this place."

"Yeah, I guess," she said. "You're pretty tall."

"How tall do you think I am?"

"I dunno, six-two?"

Clint was six feet.

"Close enough," he said. "Have you seen many men in here who are taller than me?"

"I guess one or two . . ."

"But nobody comes to mind?"

"Not right now," she said. "None of the regulars, anyway."

"I'll be in town for a while," Clint said. "If anyone comes to mind—"

"—I'll sure let ya know, honey," she said, tossing down her champagne. "Thanks for the drink."

She bounced up and hurried off to continue working the floor.

# Chapter Fifteen

A few beers and a lot of overheard conversations later and Clint still had nothing about the Tall Texan. Also, while seated there, he saw no one enter the saloon who exceeded six foot two.

He had only been in Woodriver for less than a day, so he wasn't feeling discouraged at all. He was about to pack it in and head for his hotel for the night when the sheriff came through the front door. The man went to the bar, got two beers, and then walked over to Clint's table.

"Mind if I join ya?" Mayhew asked.

"As long as one of those is for me," Clint said.

"Sure is," Mayhew said, sitting and pushing the beer over to Clint. "One's usually my limit."

That may have been the case, but Clint could see by the redness of the man's eyes that he had already had a few pulls from that whiskey bottle in his desk.

"How's your investigation goin'?" the sheriff asked.

"Slowly," Clint said. "Everybody I've spoken to seems to have the same opinion. Nobody minds that the bank was robbed, except for poor Mr. Cooke, the manager."

"I guess yer just gonna hafta keep askin' questions, then," Mayhew said.

"That's how it looks, Sheriff," Clint said. "Say, you're not making your rounds now, are you?"

Mayhew grinned.

"Guess you kin tell I hadda few, huh?"

"Yeah, kinda."

"Naw, no rounds," Mayhew said. "One beer here and then I'm goin' ta bed."

"I'm going to do the same thing," Clint said. "Can I walk you to wherever you're going? Your office, or home?"

"I don't need no nursemaid, Adams." Mayhew said, suddenly crabby. He picked up the beer mug, drained it and then slammed it down. "There! And now I'm leavin' on my own."

"Whatever you say, Sheriff," Clint said.

The lawman stood up and, on an unsteady gate, headed for the saloon door. Clint watched him stagger until he had finally made it out the door.

"He does that a lot."

Clint looked around, saw Lori standing next to his table.

"How does he keep his job?" Clint asked.

"Oh, he only gets drunk at night, just before he turns in," she said. "And it's a real quiet town. Nothin' ever happens around here."

"You had a bank robbery," Clint reminded her.

"Yeah," she said, rolling her eyes, "once, four years ago."

She moved off and he finished his beer before leaving the saloon.

***

When he entered his room, he saw the envelope on the floor, which obviously had been slipped under his door. He closed the door, picked up the envelope and opened it. In a simple, very clear handwriting it said: IF YOU WANT MORE INFORMATION ABOUT THE TALL TEXAN COME TO ROOM THREE.

Clint refolded the note. He was in room five. Room three was right across the hall from him. He wondered if this was a joke or a trap? Either way, he figured he might as well check it out. But first he went down to the front desk.

"Yes, sir?" the clerk asked.

"Who's in room three?" Clint asked.

"Room three?" the clerk repeated. "That's, uh, right across the hall from you."

"I know that," Clint said, patiently. "I want to know who rented it."

"It was a young lady named . . ." The clerk consulted the register book. ". . . Smith."

"When did she come in?"

"Just this afternoon."

"And you were here when she checked in?"

"Yes."

"What did she look like?"

"She, uh, was rather . . . plain," the clerk said.

"Did she say anything?" Clint asked. "Ask for anyone?"

"She didn't ask for you, if that's what you mean, Sir," the clerk said.

"Yes, that's what I mean."

"She didn't mention you."

"Can I see that book?"

"Of course."

Clint turned the book around. She had signed as simply SMITH, from TEXAS.

"All right." Clint said. "Thanks."

Clint went back upstairs and walked to room three. He knocked on the door, prepared to draw his weapon at a moment's notice. But when the door opened, he realized that wouldn't be necessary.

"What took you so long?" Abby West asked.

# Chapter Sixteen

"Plain?" Abby repeated. "He said I was plain?"

"I asked you what you're doing here," Clint said.

He had entered her room and shut the door before telling her what the clerk said.

"How could he say I'm plain?" She looked down at herself. "Of course, it could be he was just talking about my clothes. They *are* plain."

"Abby!" Clint snapped. "Why are you here?"

"You left San Francisco without talking to me again," she said. "That wasn't very nice of you, Clint."

"I didn't want to argue with you," Clint said.

"Very well," she said. "Let's not argue. You told me where you were going, so I followed you. But don't worry, I didn't tell anyone."

Clint took a good look at her for the first time. He still found her pretty, but she *had* dressed down for her trip from San Francisco. The shirt and trousers she was wearing were, indeed, very plain.

"You have to go back," Clint said.

"Why?"

"I work alone, Abby," he insisted.

"Okay, so work," she said. "You go your way, and I'll go mine."

"I can't work while I'm worrying about you," he explained.

"What's to worry about?" she asked. "It's not like we're huntin' a killer."

"The longer he operates, the more chance there is he's going to hurt or kill somebody," Clint said. "I don't want that to be you."

"I appreciate your concern," Abby said, "but I can take care of myself."

Clint took a deep breath and let it out slowly.

"All right," he said, "what was it you wanted to tell me about the Tall Texan?"

"What do you mean?"

"Your note, if I wanted to know more—"

"Oh, that was just to get you here," she said. "I don't know any more than I did before."

"So on top of being sneaky," he said, "you're a liar."

"I'm a woman," she said. "We're often sneaky, and sometimes we lie."

"Is there anything else?" Clint asked.

"Well, yes, one more thing," she said, turning her back to him.

"And what would that be?"

After a moment she turned back to him. She had unbuttoned her shirt and was holding it open so he could see her naked breasts. They were peach-sized, with dark nipples that were already hardening.

"Do you really think I'm plain?" she asked.

\*\*\*

After the sheriff left the saloon, he went back to his office. As he entered, the man sitting at his desk turned and spread his arms.

"Finally!" he said. "Where have you been?"

"Around," Mayhew said. "I made my rounds and then finished up at the saloon."

"And now you're drunk."

"Tipsy, is more like it," Mayhew said. "Why are you here, Jason?"

"I heard the Gunsmith's in town," Jason Boone said.

"That's true."

"What's he want?"

"What makes you think I know?" Mayhew said. "And get out of my chair."

Boone stood up so Mayhew could drop heavily onto his seat.

"So?"

"So what?" Mayhew asked, his eyes dropping to half-mast.

Boone leaned forward and snapped his fingers in the sheriff's face.

"Concentrate, Sheriff!" he shouted. "Stay awake."

"Yeah, okay!" Mayhew said. "Let's finish so I can go to sleep."

"Still sleepin' in a cell?"

"Why not? They're empty."

"What does Clint Adams want in town?" the man asked.

"You must know by now," Mayhew said. "He's lookin' for the Tall Texan."

"Why? He's not a bounty hunter."

"He's been recruited by the Pinkertons."

"The Pinkertons!" the man spat. "They've tried three or four times already."

"Well, I suppose they're tryin' again."

"And why would he start here?" Boone wondered.

"Why don't you ask him?" Mayhew said. "Maybe he'll tell you."

"You know," Boone said, thoughtfully, "that might be an idea."

## Chapter Seventeen

"Abby," Clint said, staring at her breasts, "this is not going to change my mind."

"I know that," she said, "but I want to have something to show for my trip here." She moved closer to him. "Being with you will be memorable."

"I'm flattered."

"Don't be modest," she said. "I know your reputation with the ladies." She started to unbutton his shirt, slid her hands inside. "What do you say?"

She slipped his shirt off and tossed it aside, ran her hands up his naked back.

"Well," he said, "just so it's not a complete waste."

He pulled her to him and kissed her, her hard breasts and nipples crushed to his chest.

\*\*\*

Jason Boone entered the hotel and approached the front desk.

"Yes?" the clerk asked.

"What room is Clint Adams in?"

"Mr. Adams is in room five," the clerk said.

"Thanks."

Boone started for the stairs.

"But I don't think he's in, at the moment," the clerk said, feeling he should protect an illustrious guest.

Boone stopped and turned around.

"Do you know where he is?"

"No, sir," the clerk said, which was true. He didn't know exactly where Clint Adams was, even though he suspected he was in room three.

Boone turned and came back.

"Does he eat breakfast here?" Boone asked.

"Well," the clerk said, "he did this morning."

"All right, then," Boone said. "I'll check back tomor-row mornin'."

The clerk nodded.

"Oh," Boone said, "please don't tell him that some-one was lookin' for him."

"Of course not, sir," the clerk lied. "I wouldn't think of it."

Boone nodded, and left the hotel.

***

Clint and Abby undressed each other, and then gravi-tated to the bed. He explored her tight body with his hands and mouth, bringing her to a fever pitch several times before allowing her pleasure to completely engulf her. She gasped, her body went taut, and she clung to him until the tremors passed. He removed his mouth from her crotch as she grabbed, clutching him to her.

"My God," she gasped.

"So you're not disappointed?" he asked, kissing her neck and shoulders.

"I think you've lived up to your reputation," she said. "But I don't think I'm ready to say my trip hasn't been wasted."

"Really?"

"I think," she said, pushing him off her, "you should lie on your back and let me explore the situation further."

He obeyed, rolling over and allowing her to begin her exploration of his body . . .

\*\*\*

Sheriff Grant Mayhew went to the center of the three cells in the cell block, sat and removed his boots. He thought about having another drink before turning in, but decided against it. He knew if he had another, he'd follow it with a few more, and then his condition in the morning would be unbearable.

He fluffed the flat pillow, grabbed the blanket and drew it over him as he settled down onto his back.

Before drifting off to sleep, he thought about Clint Adams' presence in Woodriver. With any luck the man would leave in a day or two, but if he stayed longer, trouble might follow.

He thought about Jason Boone, and wondered how far he might go to get Clint Adams to leave town, before . . . before . . .

. . . Mayhew drifted off to sleep.

***

After Abby had availed herself of every inch of Clint's body, she centered her attention on his swollen cock. Her ministrations had brought him to the brink several times, but she was adept at quelling a man's desire to finish. Eventually, she took him fully into her mouth and began to suck him, while running her hands up and down his thighs, or fondling his swollen testicles. And when the time came that neither of them were able to restrain him, he exploded into her mouth with a loud roar . . .

# Chapter Eighteen

"You were right," Clint said later, as he got dressed.

"About what?" Abby asked, from the bed. "About us working together, I hope."

"No," he said, "about you not being plain. There's nothing plain about you."

"A compliment from The Gunsmith?" she said. "I'll take it."

He walked to the door, then stopped.

"I assume you'll be leaving town tomorrow?"

She stretched, pulling her tight body even more taut. Clint looked away, lest he head back to the bed for another session.

"I'm tired," she said, yawning. "Can we talk about it in the morning, over breakfast?"

"Why not?" he said. "I'll meet you in the lobby at eight."

"See you then," she said, rolling over and pulling the sheet over her.

Clint left and went across the hall to his own room.

\*\*\*

Clint woke in the morning feeling pleasantly re-freshed, despite the exertions the night before with Abby West. Of course, he liked her more since having spent the time with her, but he was still determined to get her to leave town.

He washed and got dressed. As he left his room, he considered knocking on the door of room three, but decided just to meet her in the lobby.

After fifteen minutes, he figured she either wasn't coming down or had overslept. He went to the front desk.

"If a lady is looking for me would you tell her I'm already in the dining room?"

"Of course, Sir."

"Thanks."

"Oh, Mr. Adams," the clerk said, as he started away.

"Yes."

"I think I should tell you," the clerk said, "there was a man here last night looking for you."

"A man?" Clint walked back to the desk. "What man?"

"I don't know who he was," the clerk said. "He asked what room you were in, and I told him. Then I felt bad about that, so I told him you weren't in."

"And?"

"Well, he asked me if you eat breakfast here, so I told him you did yesterday morning," The clerk said. "He said he'd be back today."

"Is that all?"

"Yes, Sir."

"You didn't tell him about room three?"

"No, sir," the clerk said, "I didn't see any reason to."

"That's good," Clint said. "What's your name?"

"It's Ben, Sir."

"Thank you, Ben," Clint said. "If that man comes in looking for me again, you can tell him I'm in the dining room."

"Yes, Sir."

Clint walked across the lobby to the small dining room and got a table against the wall with no trouble. There were very few other diners present.

***

Abby West was about to leave her room to meet Clint Adams when there was a knock on her door. She had already heard Clint leave his room, so she doubted it was him. When she opened it, she found herself looking at a tall man in his thirties.

"Can I help you?"

"I don't think so," the man said, "but I think I can help you."

"Oh? How's that?"

"I understand you're lookin' for information about the Tall Texan."

"What makes you say that?" she asked.

"I'm sorry," he said, "if I'm wrong I can just—"

"No, no," she said, as he turned to walk away, "I'm not saying that."

He turned back to her.

"Then you are looking for him?"

"I'm looking for information about him," she said, "that's true."

"Then can I come in?"

"Why don't we go down to the lobby and talk," she suggested.

"No offense," he said, "but I really don't want anyone seein' us together."

"Oh?" she said. "And why would that be?"

"It's kind of complicated," he said. "But I think if you let me come in, you'll find what I have to say very interestin'."

"I have another appointment—"

"Miss West," the man said, pushing his way into the room, "this really won't take very long, at all . . ."

## Chapter Nineteen

Clint was eating a breakfast of ham-and-eggs when a man entered the dining room and looked around. He was tall, slender, in his thirties. There were still very few diners in the room, so the man walked over to Clint.

"Mr. Adams?"

"That's right."

"Do you mind if I join you?"

"That depends on who you are and what you want," Clint said.

"My name's Jason Boone," the man said. "I understand you're lookin' for the Tall Texan."

"Mr. Boone," Clint said, "have a seat. Coffee?"

"I'll take some, yeah," Boone said, sitting across from Clint.

"Tell me," Clint said, pushing a cup of coffee across to him, "are you the Tall Texan?"

"What?" The man laughed. "No, no, I didn't come here to confess."

"I just thought I'd ask," Clint said. "So, why are you here?"

Boone sipped his coffee and set the cup down.

"Please," he said, "don't let me interrupt your breakfast. Go ahead and eat."

Clint cut some ham and forked it into his mouth.

"Mr. Boone?" Clint asked. "Why are you here?"

"To help you."

"How?"

"By tellin' you you're in the wrong place, Mr. Adams," Boone said. "The man you're lookin' for isn't here."

"How do you know that?" Clint asked. "Do you know who this Tall Texan is?"

"Well, no, not really," Boone said. "But I know he's not in Woodriver."

Clint finished chewing and washed it down with a sip of coffee, then sat back.

"Tell me something, Mr. Boone."

"What's that?"

"How tall are you?"

Boone laughed.

"You think I'm the Tall Texan?" he asked. "I'm afraid not."

"So it's not you," Clint said, "and you don't know who he is, but you know he's not here in this town. Do I have that right?"

"Yes," Boone said. "Exactly."

"Well," Clint said, "thanks for the information. Now, if you don't mind, I'd like to finish my breakfast . . . alone."

"Thanks for the coffee," Boone said. "I guess you'll be leavin' town now."

"We'll see," Clint said.

Boone seemed about to say more, but changed his mind, stood and left. Clint went back to his breakfast, after which he was going to find out who the hell Jason Boone was.

***

Jason Boone left the hotel, hoping he had accomplished something. With any luck, he had left the Gunsmith in a confused state.

***

After breakfast Clint was going to leave the hotel, but he decided to check on Abby and find out why she hadn't come to breakfast. Perhaps she had simply overslept. Or maybe—and he hoped this was it—she had checked out and left town. First, he stopped at the front desk.

"No, sir," the clerk said, "the lady in room three hasn't checked out."

"Okay, thanks."

He went upstairs and knocked on the door of room three. When there was no answer he knocked again, harder this time. She might have left the hotel without checking out. He was about to walk away when he decided to try the door. When he found it unlocked, he got a bad feeling. He turned the knob and shoved the door open, gun hand ready.

The room was empty. He stepped in to look around. Bed sheets were strewn on the floor, the table and chair were lying on their sides, the chair with what looked like a freshly broken leg. Obviously someone had been dragged from the bed, after which a struggle had ensued.

A pair of empty saddlebags were lying in a corner. He checked the drawers of the chest, found some clothing there, and a .25 caliber Colt. If Abby had left the room on her own, to search for the Tall Texan, she certainly would have taken her gun.

"Damn it!" he swore.

This was exactly the reason he hadn't wanted her along. Now he had to find her, when he should have been out looking for his prey.

# Chapter Twenty

"Adams," Sheriff Mayhew said, as Clint burst into his office.

"Who or what is a Jason Boone?" Clint demanded.

"Boone?" Mayhew said. "Uh, why?"

"He came to see me this morning," Clint said. "Interrupted my breakfast to tell me I was looking in the wrong place for the Tall Texan."

"What?" the lawman said. "Boone is just . . . he sort of does odd jobs around town. I mean, he's really not anybody, uh, important."

"He's pretty tall," Clint said. "Are you sure he's not the Tall Texan?"

"What? Boone? Impossible!"

"Or is it him, and you're covering for him?"

"Why would I cover for him?" Mayhew asked. "The Tall Texan's a thief, and I'm a lawman."

"Yeah, well, everybody around here seems to think he's some kind of hero," Clint said. "And now I have a friend who's missing from the hotel."

"What do you mean, missing?"

"I mean she checked in yesterday, and now her room's been ransacked, and she's gone," Clint said.

"Maybe this Boone grabbed her before he came to see me."

"Who is she?"

"A Pinkerton."

"A female Pinkerton?"

"That's right."

"And she's workin' with you?"

"Sort of," Clint said. "Mostly she's working on her own, but right now she's missing."

"Whataya want me to do?" Mayhew asked.

"Where can I find Boone?" Clint asked. "Where's he live?"

"I dunno," Mayhew said. "How would I know?"

"But you know him."

"Well, yeah, I know 'im," the lawman said. "I see him around town. Sometimes I don't see him for days, or weeks."

"Weeks?" Clint asked. "Where does he go for weeks?"

"I dunno," Mayhew said. "He don't report to me."

"Why would he come to me and tell me I'm looking in the wrong place?" Clint asked. "Unless he's trying to throw me off the trail."

"You're askin' me a bunch of questions I dunno the answers to."

"Either he knows who the Tall Texan is," Clint said, "or it's him."

"I gotta tell ya," Mayhew said, "I don't think he's smart enough."

"Sheriff," Clint said, "I'm going to find him, and if he did anything to that girl—"

"Look," Mayhew said, "if I see 'im, I'll let you know. I'll ask around."

"The girl's name is Abby West," Clint said. "If you find her, let me know right away."

"I'll do that," the sheriff said.

Clint turned and headed for the door, then turned back.

"Sheriff, if you know who this thief is, tell him I'm not leaving here without him. And if he, or Boone, has hurt Abby West—"

"I get it, Adams," Mayhew said. "You'll kill somebody. Maybe even me."

"You?" Clint said. "Now, why would I kill a good lawman like you?"

He left before Mayhew could say anything else.

***

Back at the hotel Clint went to the desk clerk again.

"Did you see anybody go up to the second floor this morning?" he asked.

"No, Sir."

"Whether it was a guest or not," Clint added.

"Sorry, Sir," the clerk said. "Nobody."

"And you didn't see Miss West, from room three, come down, either alone or with anyone?"

"No, Sir."

"Is there a back door to the hotel?" Clint asked. "And a back stairway?"

"Yes, Sir," the clerk said, "but that door is always kept locked."

"So nobody can get in," Clint said, "but can somebody get out that way?"

"Well . . . yeah, I guess so. But if somebody goes out that way, they'd be leaving the door unlocked."

"So if we go back there now and find the door unlocked," Clint said, "somebody went out."

"Right."

"Let's go and do that, right now," Clint said.

# Chapter Twenty-One

Clint followed the young clerk down a hallway to the rear of the hotel.

"There's the door," he said, pointing.

Clint went to the door and turned the knob. It was unlocked.

"Damn it!" he snapped. "Either she went out this way, or she was taken out this way."

"By who?" the clerk asked.

"That's a good question."

Clint opened the door wide and stepped outside. The clerk stood in the doorway, watching him.

"You get deliveries from back here?"

"Once is a while."

"Today?"

"No, sir."

Clint crouched down, examined the ground.

"These wagon tracks are fresh," he said.

"A buggy?" the clerk asked.

"Heavier," Clint said. "Maybe a buckboard."

"So what now?"

"Now I get my horse and follow these tracks," Clint said. "Let's go back in."

They went back inside, locked the door, continued to the lobby.

"Do you know a man named Boone?" Clint asked, as the clerk went back around the desk.

The young man hesitated.

"You got something to tell me?" Clint asked.

"Well . . . I told you a man was askin' about you?" the clerk said.

"Yeah."

"It was Boone."

"How do you know Boone?"

The young man shrugged.

"Everybody in town knows Boone."

"Do you know where he lives?"

"No."

"How often do you see him?"

"Now and again," the clerk said. "Sometimes I don't see 'im for weeks."

If Boone was the Tall Texan, he could be away for weeks while he was pulling another job. The same was true if he was just working with the thief.

"Okay, thanks," Clint said.

"I hope you find the lady, sir," the clerk said.

"So do I."

***

Clint collected Toby from the livery stable and walked the horse around behind the hotel.

"Okay, boy," he said, mounting up, "if nothing else, we've got a trail to follow."

The wagon tracks went out onto the main street, where it got mixed in with other, older tracks. Clint was able to follow to the edge of town and out. The thing about a wagon or a buckboard was that, if you wanted the wheels to stay on, you had to ride on an established road. Taking it overland would be risking all kinds of calamity.

Of course, Clint was assuming that Abby West was in the back of this particular buckboard, hopefully tied up and not dead. If he found her dead, he was going to be livid with several people, not the least of which was Abby, herself. If he managed to find her tied up somewhere, he was going to make damn sure she headed back to San Francisco.

He followed the trail for a couple of miles, and then the buckboard did depart from the main road. But the route it took had been taken many times before, thus a rough, bumpy road lay ahead. Obviously, this wagon had been back and forth this way other times.

When he spotted a shack ahead, he reined in, dismounted and tied the Tobiano to a bush. He could not yet trust the horse not to wander away, as he had often done with his previous mounts, Duke and Eclipse. The To-biano still had a lot to learn.

He approached the shack on foot, moving carefully. There was no sign of the buckboard or a horse, but that didn't mean someone wasn't inside. It just meant the buckboard had been here and gone.

As he got closer, he moved around to the side, rather than approach the structure head on. It had the look of a line shack, probably just enough room inside. There was a window in the front wall, and the side wall, although no glass. When he reached the side, he flattened his back against the wall and waited, listening for any sounds from inside. When he didn't hear any, he decided to risk a look in the side window.

There wasn't much inside beyond a cot with some-thing on it, covered by a blanket. He decided to risk going in and went to the front door. It was flimsy, certainly not locked, so he opened it.

# Chapter Twenty-Two

He hesitated, wondering if whoever was under the blanket was tied up, sleeping, or dead? There was only one way to find out. He approached the cot, grabbed the blanket and pulled it off. Beneath it he found Abby West, trussed up, gagged and alive. Her eyes were open very wide as she stared up at him. When she recognized him, he saw relief there, and then she started trying to talk.

He removed the gag from her mouth.

"Thank God!" she said. "I thought that sonofabitch was coming back to kill me."

"Relax, you're fine now," he said, untying her and helping her sit up. She rubbed her wrists while he untied her ankles.

"Was it Boone?" Clint asked.

"Who's Boone?" she asked. "Some man knocked on my door, said he had information about the Tall Texan. I was dumb enough to let him in. Next thing I know he hit me with something. When I came to, I was over his shoulder being tossed into the back of a buckboard."

"He didn't say his name?"

"No. He didn't talk to me at all, after I let him in," she said. She looked around. "Where the hell are we?"

"It looks like an old line shack," he said. "Come on, let's get you out of here."

He helped her to her feet and outside, where they walked to his horse.

"Didn't you wonder where I was when I didn't come to breakfast?" she demanded.

"I thought maybe you overslept," he said. "Besides, I had a visitor."

"What visitor?"

"I'm thinking it was the man who grabbed you," he said. "His name was Jason Boone."

"What's he look like?" she asked.

"Tall, slender, thirties—"?

"Sounds like him," she said, then her eyes widened. "Tall? Is he—"

"He says he's not," Clint said, "but he came to tell me I'm looking in the wrong place."

"I don't know why he grabbed me and tied me up," she said, "but that sure doesn't make it sound like we're looking in the wrong place, does it?"

"No," he said, "it doesn't."

He mounted up, then reached down and pulled her up behind him.

"Where is this guy?" she asked, as they started back to town.

"I don't know," Clint said, "but we're going to find him."

"*We* are?" she asked.

"Yes," he said. "I think you're entitled to stick around now, don't you?"

"I thought that before I got kidnapped!"

\*\*\*

Clint rode directly to Sheriff Mayhew's office.

"I want Jason Boone arrested!" Abby snapped, as they entered.

"And who are you?" Mayhew asked.

"This is Abby West," Clint said, "the lady Jason Boone abducted, tied up and tossed into an old line shack."

Mayhew pointed at her.

"The lady Pinkerton?"

"That's right," she said, "and the Pinkerton Detective Agency doesn't take it lightly when one of their agents is attacked."

Abby's eyes flashed from her smudged face as she waved her dirty hands at the sheriff.

"I don't know where Boone is," Mayhew told her, "but I'll find him, Ma'am."

"You do that!" she snapped. Then she looked down at herself, turned up her nose and turned to Clint. "I need a hot bath."

"I'm sure you can get it at the hotel," he said. "You do that while I look for Boone."

"If you find him first, Adams," Mayhew said, "don't kill 'im."

"If I find him first, I'm going to make him take me to the Tall Texan."

"I still think you're way off about that," Sheriff Mayhew said. "Even if he's from here, why would someone like that, who's built up a big reputation for himself, wanna live around here?"

"I don't know, Sheriff," Clint said, "but when I find him, I'll ask him."

Clint and Abby left the sheriff's office.

"I'm going to take my horse to the livery," he said. "You go to the hotel, arrange your bath, and then go to your room and get your gun. Keep it with you at all times. I don't want you getting kidnapped again."

"You and me both!" she said.

# Chapter Twenty-Three

Clint decided to walk Abby to the hotel before taking the Tobiano to the livery stable.

"Get that gun!" he snapped as she went into the lobby.

"I know!"

As he left the hotel, he still wished she had never followed him to Woodriver. But now that she was there, he was going to have to deal with her.

He walked the Tobiano to the livery, handed him over to the grateful hostler, and then headed for the saloon, which was empty that early in the day.

"Hope you don't mind me making you work so early, Garrett," Clint said, "but I'll take a beer."

"No problem, friend," the man said. "There ya go!"

Clint grabbed the beer and drank half of it down.

"More trail dust?" the bartender asked.

"That and anger," Clint said.

"Angry drinkin' leads to gettin' drunk," Garrett said.

"Don't worry about that," Clint said. "I'm just having the one."

The bartender leaned on the bar.

"Who you mad at?" he asked.

"You know Jason Boone?" Clint asked.

"Oh yeah, I know Boone," the bartender said. "He stops in here when he's in town."

"Let me ask you something," Clint said. "What do you think of the possibility that he's the Tall Texan?"

"Boone?" Garrett stood up straight and laughed. "He's not smart enough."

"I guess I'm starting to believe that, too," Clint said. "He did two very dumb things just today, one of which was kidnapping."

"Kidnapping?" the bartender said. "That don't sound like Boone."

"Just how well do you know him?" Clint asked.

"As well as I know anybody who comes in here and drinks," Clint said.

"So you don't know where he lives?"

"Not a clue," Garrett said.

"You know anybody who would know?" Clint asked. "Anybody who's friends with him?"

"Sorry."

"That's okay," Clint said. "I'll find him."

"You gonna kill 'im?"

Clint finished his beer and said, "That's going to be up to him."

***

Sheriff Mayhew sat at his desk and wondered what the hell was wrong with Jason Boone? Was it possible he knew where the Tall Texan was? Or could he himself have been the thief? Mayhew doubted that. Boone just wasn't smart enough for that. But kidnapping? Mayhew didn't think Boone was that dumb.

He'd been telling Adams the truth. He had no idea where Boone lived. He also didn't know if the man had any friends in town. So as far as finding him, he didn't know the first place to start.

Maybe Clint Adams was right. Maybe he was the one who ought to find Boone and set the man straight.

As for the Tall Texan, if he did live in the area, he probably knew by now that the Gunsmith was looking for him. Maybe a Gunsmith/Tall Texan showdown was going to put Woodriver on the map.

\*\*\*

Clint had a second beer.

"Does this town have a mayor? A Town Council?"

"In name only," Garrett said.

"What's that mean?"

"This is a small place," the barkeep said. "Everybody sort of goes their own way and makes their own rules."

"But you have a lawman," Clint said.

"You've met Mayhew," the bartender said. "What kind of lawman do you think he is?"

"I get your point."

"I'll give ya some advice," Garrett said, "if ya want it."

"I'll take it," Clint said. He trusted bartenders more than anybody in a town.

"If you're gonna find the Tall Texan around here, nobody's gonna help ya," the bartender said. "You're on your own. But watch your back."

"I always do," Clint told him, "but thanks. You think people won't help me, but they might try to stop me?"

"I wouldn't 've thought that," the bartender said, "but what you tell me about Boone, he's gettin' himself involved. I'm just wonderin' who else would do the same thing?"

"Are there any would-be gunnies in the area?" Clint asked.

"Nah," the bartender said, "not that I've seen. Folks around here are relaxed and mind their own business . . . usually. But you bein' here, and the reason you're here? It might make a difference."

"I'll keep all that in mind," Clint said. "Thanks."

# Chapter Twenty-Four

Clint left the saloon and walked back to his hotel. Ben was behind the desk.

"Has Miss West had her bath?" he asked.

"Yes, sir," the clerk said. "She's back upstairs in her room."

"Good. Thanks. Anyone else come in here looking for me?"

"No."

"Well, if they do, tell them I'm in my room."

"Yessir."

Clint went upstairs to the second floor and knocked on the door of room three. When Abby opened it, she looked fresh and clean, and smelled like soap. She was wearing a dress that showed a bit of her cleavage.

"You won't want to go out in that frock," he told her. "You'd be certain not to be taken as plain."

"It's all I have until my clothes dry," she said. "They were as filthy as I was." She indicated her shirt and trousers, which were draped over the table and now three-legged chair to dry.

He entered and closed the door.

"Where's your gun?"

She walked to the bed and showed him the gun on the night table.

"Next time you answer your door, have it in your hand!" he snapped.

"All right!" she said. Then her face softened. "You're really worried about me?"

"You bet I am," he said. "Pinkerton's going to blame me if you get killed."

"Is that the only reason you're worried about me?"

"You're supposed to be able to take care of yourself," he scolded her. "How could you let yourself be taken like that?"

"He caught me off guard," she argued. "It won't happen again."

"See that it doesn't," he said. "I've got better things to do than go looking for you."

"What are you so mad about?" she asked.

"Nothing," he said. "Just don't get yourself killed, that's all."

"I'll do my best."

He headed for the door.

"Where are you going now?" she asked.

"Back to what I was supposed to be doing before you got here," he said. "I'm going to find the Tall Texan."

"How sure are you he's here?"

"Not sure at all," Clint said, "but I'm becoming convinced that he's from here, and that's a start."

"Well, wait for me—"

"Not in that dress," he said.

"My clothes are almost dry!"

Clint looked over at them, as they dripped water on the floor.

"I don't think so," Clint said. "I'll come back and get you at supper time."

"But Clint—"

"Until then, stay inside," he said, "and don't open the door for anyone but me."

"Clint—" she tried to argue, but he was out the door.

***

Clint wondered about going back to the line shack. Would there be anything there that could tell him something about Boone? And if Boone hadn't yet returned there, might he return to check on his kidnap victim?

He made the decision to go back, went to the livery for his horse, again.

"I hope you're comin' back with him," the hostler said.

"I'm not ready to leave town for good yet, old timer," he said. "We'll be back."

The old man rubbed his hands together with glee as Clint rode out.

***

He rode to the line shack and dismounted right out in front. He tied off the Tobiano and went back inside. He checked underneath the cot, looked around the interior, but found nothing of any use. He decided to give it some time to see if Boone would return, so he went outside and walked the Tobiano out of sight.

He circled the horse, put him in a comfortable position against one wall of the shack. It was a tight fit for the two of them, but he needed the animal to be out of sight, but safe.

"Just relax, fella," he said, stroking the Tobiano's neck. "We won't be in here long."

He went to the front window, wishing he had something to sit on, but decided to simply lean there and stare out, hoping Boone would appear before dusk came. If he didn't, then maybe his plan had been to leave Abby there until she starved to death.

# Chapter Twenty-Five

As it started to get dark, Clint decided to give up for the day. He walked over to Toby, was about to lead him away from the shack when he felt something beneath his feet. He stomped his foot and realized there were some loose floorboards. That wasn't odd in a rundown shack like that, but he bent over to check anyway. He found two of the boards loose and removed them both, revealing something secreted beneath the floor. He reached in and came out with a burlap sack that was tied tight. He undid it and peered inside before sticking his hand in and coming out with cash. He immediately took this to mean that these were proceeds from some of the Tall Texan's robberies. And if they were hidden under the floor of this shack, Jason Boone either was the thief, or knew him. But it now seemed obvious to Clint that he was right to begin his search in Woodriver.

He put the cash back in the sack, returned it to where he found it, and replaced the floorboards. He probably should have remained in there all night, waiting for one man or the other to show up, but he thought it better to do his waiting during the day.

He walked the Tobiano out of the shack, mounted up and rode back to town.

\*\*\*

"You found him?" Abby said, excitedly.

"I found a hiding place for the loot from his robberies," Clint said.

"But he'll be coming back for it."

"That's what I figure."

"Or hope."

"No," Clint said, "someone will come back for the money. Whoever it is, they'll take me to the thief—or be the thief, himself."

"So then we just have to wait," Abby said.

"Yes," Clint said. "I'll have to camp near the shack and watch."

"We," she said. "My clothes are dry, now. You can't keep me away."

"Very well," Clint said, "we'll camp and wait, starting tomorrow."

"So what about tonight?"

"Right now, let's go and get something to eat."

"That suits me," she said. "Do you know a good place?"

"I've been taking my meals here, in the hotel's dining room, rather than go out and look for another place."

"Fine," she said. "Let's go."

They left the room and went downstairs.

\*\*\*

As with his previous meals, there were very few diners in the room. Clint walked Abby to a back table, and the wizened old waiter came over.

"Welcome back, Sir," he said. "What can I get for you and your guest?"

"Steaks and beer," Clint said, "and everything that comes with it."

"Right away."

"What about after this?" Abby said. "What do we do with the rest of the night?"

"Go back to your room and rest," Clint said.

"We both go back to my room—" she started.

"No," he said, "you go to your room and I go to mine and we rest—and stay alert and alive. That reminds me, do you have your gun on you?"

"I do," she said. "It's in my belt."

"Good. Maybe tomorrow you can show me if you can use it."

"I can usually hit what I aim at," she told him.

"We'll see."

The waiter brought their dinners and they dug in. Clint had had better steaks over the years, but he'd also had worse. Abby seemed to like hers, as she gave the plate all her attention. She finished eating well ahead of Clint.

"You always eat that fast?" he asked.

"I was brought up in an orphanage," she said. "If you didn't eat fast, and guard your food, sometimes you didn't eat at all."

"That must've been a very tough way to grow up," he commented.

"Tough is right," she said. "It made me strong, which you ain't seen yet, but you will."

They finished their meal, then Clint paid the bill and walked with Abby to her door.

"Remember what I said," he told her. "Get some rest but stay alert."

"And stay alive," she said. "I've got it. Good night, Clint."

"Good night."

He stood in front of her door until he heard the lock, then turned and went to his own room.

## Chapter Twenty-Six

Jason Boone entered the small town of Tonka, Texas as it was getting dark. It was even smaller than Woodriver, with only a trading post and a stable. He reined in his horse in front of the trading post and went inside. The man behind the counter recognized him and ignored him. Boone walked through the store to the back room. A man sitting on a carton, with a bandana covering the lower half of his face, his long legs stretched out in front of him, was waiting.

"It's about time," he said.

"I had to make sure Clint Adams didn't follow me," Boone said. He looked around for someplace to sit, didn't find one, so he just stood.

"Clint Adams is in Woodriver?" the other man asked. "What's he want?"

"What do you think he wants?" Boone asked. "He's lookin' for the Tall Texan."

The man frowned.

"What the hell made him go there?" he said. "If he's huntin', he should've gone to Wichita, where the last job was pulled."

"He decided to do it different and start where it all began."

The man considered that.

"I gotta say," he finally commented, "that may've been pretty smart."

"He's also got help with him."

"What kind of help?"

"A female Pinkerton."

"What?" The man laughed. "What does he think she's gonna do?"

"Well, nothin', now," Boone said.

"Whataya mean?"

"I grabbed her."

"You what?"

"I, uh, kidnapped her."

"And what did you do with her?"

"I put her in the line shack," Boone answered.

"What?" the man exploded. "The same shack where we have the money hidden?"

"Well . . . yeah."

"So if he looks for her—and he will—and finds her, he's also gonna find the money."

"No, he won't," Boone said. "It's under the floor."

"Boone," the man said, "why are you such an idiot?"

"Whataya mean?"

"You've gotta move that money," the man said. "Tomorrow."

"And what about the girl?" Boone asked.

"Get rid of 'er!"

"You mean kill 'er?"

"I mean get rid of 'er," the man said again. "I ain't gonna tell you how, Boone. Don't make me start thinkin' I picked the wrong man for this job." He reached down and came up with a burlap sack like the one under the floorboards. He tossed it to Boone. "There's the proceeds from the last two jobs. Make sure everybody gets a fair share, and you put the rest away with the money you take from the shack. Find someplace good to hide it, this time."

"You want me to hand it out, even with the Gunsmith in town?" Boone asked.

"Nobody's gonna tell him what's goin' on," the man said. "Just be smart about it, Jason. Can you do that?"

"Sure," Boone said, "sure, I can do it."

"Then get out of here."

Boone started for the door, then stopped.

"What are we gonna do about the Gunsmith?" Boone asked. "What if he don't leave?"

"If he keeps snoopin', let me know," the man said. "I may have to ride in and take care of him myself."

"Okay."

"But before I do that," the man went on, "you can get help, right?"

"Oh, yeah," Boone said, "I got guys I can call on for the job."

"Then we'll try that first," the man said. "Let me know what happens. Leave me a message here, as usual."

"Okay," Boone said. "I'll get it done, I swear."

"Get goin', Boone."

Boone left the back room, went through the store to the outside, mounted up and rode off.

When he had ridden away, the man came out of the back room and accepted a glass of whiskey from the old man behind the counter.

"Thanks, Pop."

"That boy's gonna get you killed," the old man said. "Wait and see."

"I can handle him, Pop."

The older man shook his head.

"He's just so dumb," he said. "He's gonna get you killed, boy," the man repeated.

# Chapter Twenty-Seven

When Clint woke the next morning, it was with the feeling that he should have taken the money from beneath the floorboards of the shack. It would certainly have shaken somebody up when they found it was gone.

When he knocked on Abby's door, she answered as if she'd been standing on the other side, waiting.

"Breakfast?" she asked.

"A quick one," Clint said. "I've decided we should get to that shack and take that money."

"And do what with it?" she asked.

"Sit on it," Clint said. "I want them to panic."

"You mean Boone and the Texan?"

"I hope that's who I mean," Clint said. "I don't want to find out anybody else is involved."

"I have a theory," she said, as they walked down the hall.

"Really," he said. "Why don't you tell it to me over breakfast?"

They got downstairs, sat at the same table and ordered from the same waiter, who wasn't busy at all.

"Does anybody else ever eat here?" Abby asked him.

"Other guests," he said, "when we have other guests."

"And where do the townspeople eat?" she asked.

"There's a café at the other end of town that does a brisk business for breakfast and supper."

She looked at Clint.

"Maybe we could try that tomorrow?" she said.

"Why? This is fine." He looked at the waiter. "Flapjacks for both of us."

"It might help with my theory," she said, as the waiter walked away.

"And just what is your theory?" he asked.

She leaned forward anxiously.

"What if the whole town is in on it?" she asked.

"What?"

"The whole town," she said, "helpin' him, coverin' for him."

Clint stared at her.

"What's wrong?" she asked.

"I like it," he said.

"Really?"

"Yes," Clint said. "I've been thinking everybody's simply pleased with having him come from here, but if they're all in on it, that explains a lot."

"Like what?"

"Like the money under the floorboards," Clint said. "It doesn't look like the thief goes out and spends his booty, does it?"

"What do'ya think he does with it?" she asked.

"Well," Clint said, "there's that Robin Hood nonsense."

"Who?"

"You know, steal from the rich and give to the poor?"

She shook her head.

"I don't understand."

"You've never read Robin Hood?" Clint asked.

"I'm afraid we didn't do very much readin' in the orphanage," she said.

"Well," Clint said, "there's this thief named Robin Hood who lives in Sherwood Forest . . ."

***

After breakfast they headed for the livery stable.

"We'll have to get you a horse for the ride to the shack," he said. "Unless you'd prefer a buggy?"

"I can ride, thank you," she told him.

"Good."

When they got to the livery Clint rented her a mare, and had the hostler saddle her while he saddled the Tobiano. Together, they rode out to the line shack.

When they arrived, they dismounted and he told her, "Stay here and keep an eye out."

"Right."

Clint went inside, pried up the loose floorboards and pulled out the sack, then replaced the boards. Outside he showed her the contents.

"That's a lot of cash," she said. "Who do we return it to?"

"That's not for me to say," Clint said. "There have been plenty of robberies and there's not enough here to pay them all back."

"So what do we do with it?"

"We hold onto it for a while," Clint said. "Meanwhile let's get away from here before someone comes along."

They mounted up and rode a short distance before dismounting and hiding the horses.

"We can watch the shack from here," Clint said.

"For how long?" she asked.

"Until somebody comes along."

She stared at him.

"Or until supper," he added, "whichever comes first."

114

# Chapter Twenty-Eight

They took turns, one standing and watching, the other sitting. As it was getting on toward afternoon, Clint was starting to become impatient with the sitting, when Abby hissed at him.

"Somebody's comin'!" she whispered.

He got to his feet and stood next to her, so they could both watch. A lone rider was approaching the shack, and Clint recognized him as Boone.

"That's the man who grabbed me!" Abby said, angrily. Clint had to hold her by the shoulders to keep her from charging the man.

"Easy," he said. "It's also the guy who warned me off, so let's see what he's going to do."

Reluctantly, Abby settled back to continue watching.

Boone dismounted and went inside. After a few minutes they heard a racket inside, as if someone was wrecking the place, and then Boone came staggering out. He had his hat in his hand and was running the other hand through his hair. When he started looking around, the two of them ducked back out of sight. When they peered out again, Boone was standing there staring at the ground.

"What's he doin'?" she asked.

"He's wondering what to do," Clint said.

"And what's in that sack hangin' from his saddle?"

"Probably more money," Clint said.

"Which means . . . he met with the Tall Texan," she said, excitedly.

"He was probably going to add that money to the stash in the shack," Clint said. "But with that money gone, he's going to have to decide to meet with him again, to let him know what's happened."

"Will he?" she asked. "Or will he try to find out himself?"

"I guess we'll have to wait and see," Clint said.

While they watched, Boone put his hat back on and, shaking his head, mounted up and rode off in the direction of town.

"He's headin' back to Woodriver," she said.

"He wants to try and figure this out," Clint said. "Come on, we better get back. He just might come looking for me."

"To ask you about the missin' money?" she asked.

"To feel me out, at least," Clint said, "see if I'm the one who took it."

As they mounted up, she asked, "What will you tell 'im?"

"I don't know yet," he said. "I've got some figuring to do myself."

***

They returned their horses to the hostler and asked him if anyone else had ridden in.

"You're the onliest ones who rid out, an' the onliest ones who rid back," he told them.

"Thanks," Clint said.

As they left the livery Abby asked, "Do you think he rode right out to meet with the thief?"

"No," Clint said, "I think he's probably got his own place where he keeps his horse."

"So we need to know where he lives."

"I've asked around, and nobody seems to know," Clint said, "or they're not saying."

"So where are we goin' now?" she asked.

"How about a drink?"

"I thought you'd never ask."

***

They entered the Victory Saloon and went straight to the bar. There were several men in the place, but they were all paying attention to their drinks.

117

"Help you folks?" the bartender asked.

"Two beers," Clint said.

"Comin' up."

When he set the beers in front of them, he asked, "Any luck?"

"With what?" Clint asked.

The man shrugged and replied, "With what you came here to do."

"It's kind of hard to have luck when the whole town's against you," Clint said.

"That what you figure?" the bartender asked.

"It's not just what I figure," Clint said, "it's what makes sense."

"Well then," the man said, "I guess the question is, how can you go against a whole town?"

"I guess that is the question," Clint said. "You got an answer?"

"Me?" the man said. "I'm just a bartender. I got no answers for anybody. I just listen."

He moved on down the bar to listen to somebody else.

"So you like my theory," Abby said to Clint.

"More and more," he said, sipping his beer.

# Chapter Twenty-Nine

"It's gone!" Boone said, bursting into the office.

Henry Cooke looked up from his desk in surprise.

"You're not supposed to come here!" he hissed. "Close the door!"

Boone slammed the door, then turned to face Cooke again.

"It's all gone!" he said, again.

"What's gone?" the bank manager asked.

"The money," Boone said. "The cash we've been hoarding."

"I thought you had that cash hidden away?" Cooke said.

"I did," Boone said. "And it's gone."

"But . . . how?"

"There's only one way I can think of," Boone said. "Clint Adams must've taken it."

"And what's that?" Cooke asked, pointing to the bag in Boone's hand.

"This is the latest take," Boone said. "I just got it from . . . him."

"I'll take that," Cooke said, reaching out. Boone handed him the bag. "I'll see this gets to the right people."

"But what about . . . the rest?" Boone whispered.

"If Adams has the money we've been hiding," Cooke said, "then he's going to have to be taken care of. Didn't *he* tell you that?"

"He did."

"Did he tell you how?"

"No, he just said take care of it."

"Well," Cooke said, "we know what that means, don't we?"

"But, Mr. Cooke . . . *he's* never shot anyone."

"But in this situation, dealing with the Gunsmith, how do you think he wants you to handle it? Is there another way to deal with a killer?"

"No," Boone said, "I guess not."

"Do you know some men?" Cooke asked.

"That's the same thing *he* asked me," Boone said. "Yeah, I know some."

"Then I suggest you take care of it, Boone," Cooke said. "We've been putting that money away for a reason, haven't we?"

"Yeah, we have."

"And I, for one, don't intend to just stand by and lose it," Cooke said. "And I'm sure, neither does *he*."

"Yeah, right," Boone said. "Okay, I'll handle it."

As Boone turned and headed for the door Cooke asked, "Boone, did you, uh, see him this time?"

"No," Boone said, "he kept his face hidden."

"And if you don't get this done," the manager asked, "will he step up?"

"Yeah, I think so."

"The Tall Texan against the Gunsmith," Cooke said. "That might be interesting."

"But he ain't gonna wanna step out into the open unless he has to," Boone pointed out.

"I get that, Boone," Cooke said. "Believe me, I get that." He touched the bag of money on his desk. "I'll see to this, and you see to that."

"Right," Boone said. "Right."

"Make sure you go out the back way."

Boone nodded and left.

In addition to the bank safe outside his office, Cooke had a safe behind his desk. He opened it now and put the bag of money inside, then closed it. He'd divvy it up later at night, when nobody was around, and then deliver it to each of the waiting businesses in town. Woodriver would have died out as a town years ago, if not for the generosity of the Tall Texan. There was no way they could afford to let Clint Adams change that. No way at all.

\*\*\*

Clint thought Boone might show up at the Victory Saloon, in need of a drink, but he forgot that the general store across the way also served liquor. Could he have gone over there? He would have to check.

Whatever the case, wherever he went, it was likely he would end up, sooner or later, in the Victory. He could decide to go into hiding from Clint, but that wouldn't get him back the money he had managed to lose from that sack. After all, he was going to have to figure that Clint had not only freed Abby but taken the money. He was going to have to come looking for the money, only he might not come alone.

According to everything Clint had heard about Woodriver, there were no guns for hire there. That didn't mean Boone wouldn't import them from somewhere else.

"I think I better take you back to your room," he said to Abby.

"But . . . why?"

He put his hand on her shoulder.

"Finish your beer, and I'll tell you on the way."

# Chapter Thirty

Abby complained all the way back to the hotel and up to her room.

"You told me to carry my gun everywhere, and I am," she said, as they entered her room.

"I know," he said, "I'd just feel better if you stayed here while I looked for Boone."

"Or he looks for you, is that it?" she asked. "You're tryin' to keep me out of the line of fire?"

"Yes," he said, "that's what I'm trying to do. I think if Boone comes for me, he may not come alone."

"Well," she said, "if you want me to stay here, you're gonna have to give me a better reason."

"Like what?"

She charged him then, grabbed him and kissed him fiercely.

"Abby—"

"I'm not stayin' in this room unless you take me to bed," she said. "Take it or leave it."

He stared at her for a few moments, then said, "I'll take it."

"Good," she said, reaching for his gunbelt, "then let's start with getting rid of this."

***

When Boone left the bank, he mounted his horse, which he had left by the back door. He had already decided who he was going to recruit to take care of Clint Adams. All he had to do now was ride all afternoon to get to the nearby town of Ableton, which was the antithesis of Woodriver. You couldn't walk down the street there without bumping into a would-be gunny. There was no law, and the only thing that would keep Boone alive was the promise of money.

He stayed to the alleys and back streets and left Woodriver without being seen.

***

Henry Cooke sat behind his desk, satisfied that the bag of proceeds was in his private safe. He hadn't counted the contents of the bag, but he was sure it held more than was presently sitting in the bank safe.

Once the teller, Bates, and the clerk, Mrs. Leeds, went home, he would transfer the money from his safe to the bank safe, and into the account books for the various Woodriver businesses that were on the Tall Texan's list. Then the remainder would go into his own account, which no one—not the Texan, not Boone—was aware of. And he was going to have to leave less money with Boone, if the buffoon was just going to lose it.

He didn't know how much longer this arrangement could continue. The Tall Texan would be caught, eventually, or simply give up his life of crime before he was caught or killed. And when that did happen, the business owners of Woodriver were going to be on their own. And Henry Cooke was going to have to leave town and make his way somewhere else—hopefully, with a wallet full of cash.

*** 

Clint and Abby undressed each other and fell onto her bed. He was determined that they wouldn't do this again, especially not if they were going to work together, but if this was the only way he could get her to stay in her room, so be it. It was certainly more pleasant than arguing with her.

When he got her on the bed, he pinned her on her back and kissed his way down until he was between her legs. He licked her until she was gushing and groaning, and then mounted her, driving his hard cock inside of her. Her eyes went wide and, just for a moment, he was aware that she had stopped breathing, but then she let the air out of her lungs with a loud gasp. After that she bit her lip while he slid in and out of her and managed not to scream when he exploded inside of her.

"There," he said, breathlessly, "hopefully that'll keep you inside for a while."

As he started to get off the bed she scrambled to her knees and wrapped her arms around him.

"Not so fast," she said, pulled him back down on the bed . . .

\*\*\*

Abby rode Clint until he was engorged and then she did something with her vagina that felt like she was gripping him, and he exploded again, more forcefully than the time before.

"Where did you learn that?" he asked her, when he got his breath back.

She snuggled up alongside him and said, "I worked a case once where I had to go undercover in a whore-house."

"Abby!"

She laughed.

"Those girls taught me a lot of things," she said, as he got out of bed and began to dress. "Maybe I'll show you something else."

"Not til this is all over," he told her, strapping on his gun. "After all, I'm going to need all my strength."

Her laughter followed him down the hall.

# Chapter Thirty-One

"I've got it figured," Clint said to Sheriff Mayhew.

"Have you?"

"Everybody's covering for him," Clint said. "You all know who he is."

Mayhew laughed. He had been drinking coffee when Clint came barging into his office.

"That's what you mean when you say you got it figured?" he asked. "Believe me, Adams, nobody in this town could point him out to you if he was walkin' down the street."

"I don't believe you," Clint said.

"Then shoot me," Mayhew said. "I can't tell you a thing."

"You can tell me about Boone," Clint said.

"What about him?"

"He picks up the money from the Tall Texan and brings it to town," Clint said. "I know he's been hiding some of it. What does he do with the rest?"

"Are you mad?" Mayhew said. "Why would the Tall Texan give Boone the money he steals?"

"That's what I'm asking you, Sheriff," Clint said. "I've already found the money he's been hiding."

"Where?"

"The same place he put Miss West when he kidnapped her," Clint said. "A small line shack just outside of town. The money was under the floorboards."

"How much was there?"

"I didn't count it."

"What are you gonna do with it?" Mayhew asked.

"I don't know," Clint said. "If I can find more, I can return some to each of the places that he robbed."

"That's crazy," Mayhew said. "You'd never be able to track them all down."

"I can try," Clint said, "but that'll come later."

"Where's the money now?"

"In a safe place," Clint said. "Somebody with a gun is sitting on it."

"Shouldn't you put it in the bank?"

"Not the bank in this town," Clint said. "I'm not convinced the manager's not in on all this."

"But our bank was robbed," Mayhew reminded him.

"Not of very much money," Clint said. "I'm still thinking that was his practice run."

"Well," Mayhew said, "if you've taken this money you found and hidden it, don't you think the thief will come lookin' for it?"

"I hope he does," Clint said. He was, in fact, hoping that Sheriff Mayhew would tell the thief about it.

"If you're thinkin' of forcin' some kind of shoot-out between you and him—"

"I'm not forcing anything," Clint said. "I want to take him in and recover as much of the money he stole as possible. The only problem is, I've got a whole town working against me."

"That's a silly notion," the lawman said.

"This can end peaceably, Sheriff," Clint said. "Just tell me where Boone or the thief is. Tell me who the Tall Texan is."

"I told you," Mayhew said, "I don't know."

"And you're going to stick to that?"

"It's the truth!"

"Sorry," Clint said, "but I haven't encountered very much truth since I arrived in this town."

"I don't know what to tell ya," Sheriff Mayhew said.

"You're stonewalling me, Sheriff," Clint said, "but that's okay, because I'm not leaving until I get what I want."

Clint turned and left before the lawman could respond.

***

Clint wasn't sure about his next move. He hated to consider it, but he might just have to wait until Boone or the Tall Texan made a move to come for their money. There was no telling how long that might take.

\*\*\*

Boone rode into Abelton after dark. As he entered the Northern Saloon, he saw just the men he was hoping to see.

"Hey, Boone," one of them said. "What brings you here?"

"I'm buyin' drinks," Boone said to the three men. "Beers?"

"Yeah!" they all agreed.

Boone went to the bar, got four beers and struggled to carry them all to the table without spilling them.

"There ya go," he said. "Mind if I sit?"

"Yer buyin', you can sit," another man said.

"I gotta hear this," the first man said, grinning. "Why you buyin' drinks, Boone?"

"Yeah," another man said, "this is kinda unusual."

"No, it ain't," Boone said. "I've bought drinks before."

"Only when you want something," the first man said. "What is it, this time? Your Tall Texan buddy want another favor?"

The three men laughed.

"That guy kills me," one said. "He's got some act."

"Okay, quiet down," the first man said. "Let Boone talk."

"Okay," Boone said, "so you guys have heard of the Gunsmith, right . . ."

# Chapter Thirty-Two

The quiet of the street the next morning held no warning. The streets of Woodriver were quiet that day. This was no different as Clint stepped from the hotel.

He had breakfast with Abby and told her, once again, to stay in the hotel.

"What good is my gun going to do here?" she asked.

"That depends," Clint said, "on whether or not somebody comes into the hotel looking for you."

"And what happens if somebody is out there looking for you?" she asked.

"I'm afraid I'm counting on that," he said.

"You're going to put yourself out there as bait?"

"You just have to stay in your room, keep your gun at hand, and keep that money under your bed."

"But—"

"No matter what happens," Clint said, "no matter what you hear, don't come out."

"You think it'll happen today?"

"I'm hoping," he said.

When he stepped from the hotel he stopped, lifted his chin and felt the breeze on his face. He looked up and down the street and felt that the quiet was not like the quiet of the day before.

And when he saw faces in some of the windows, looking out, waiting, he knew. His choice now was to remain in front of the hotel or put himself out on the street in the open.

He made up his mind and stepped into the street.

\*\*\*

Boone made sure he was nowhere near Woodriver. He gave the men instructions, and was leaving it to them to handle Clint Adams and get the money back. Once that was done, they were to bring it to the line shack.

Nobody would ever suspect that he would hide it there again.

\*\*\*

Unlike Clint's room, Abby's offered her a view of the main street. She went to the window and looked out. The street was empty, but the street was always empty. Then she saw him.

Clint was out in the open, like a staked goat. She picked up her gun and held it tightly in both hands.

\*\*\*

Once Clint was sure somebody was coming for him, it remained to be seen whether they would try to bushwhack him or step out and face him. He wondered if Boone or the Tall Texan himself would be among them.

The answer came moments later, as a man stepped out into the street, followed by another. Then Clint looked the other way, saw two more. They were getting ready to catch him in a crossfire. Four wasn't so bad, but if more appeared, the situation would change from dangerous to dire.

\*\*\*

From her window, Abby saw two of the men in the street. She didn't know if there were more, but she didn't like the two-to-one odds she was seeing. With her gun, she hurriedly left the room to run downstairs.

\*\*\*

Sheriff Mayhew was watching the action from his window. He knew this was Boone's doing and, by extension, the Tall Texan's. For that reason, he had to stay where he was and not get involved.

\*\*\*

Clint could see the sheriff's office from where he stood and saw Mayhew's face in the window. The lawman was just going to watch, not take part.

His eyes swept the streets, the doorways, the rooftops, looking for more men. Then he noticed Abby standing at the door of the hotel, with her gun in her hand.

Slowly, he crossed the street then stood next to her. The four men remained where they were.

"What are you doing?" he demanded.

"I thought you'd need help."

"You're supposed to be watching the money," Clint said. "I'm guessing they'll send somebody to our rooms to look for it. That's where you come in."

"But you need help here," she said.

"I've got this under control, Abby," he told her. "Now you get back up to your room and lock the door."

"Oh, all right," she said, exasperated, and went back into the hotel.

# Chapter Thirty-Three

Clint turned and looked both ways on the street. The four men stood their ground. They were all wearing side arms, two in holsters, and two tucked into their belts.

He knew he was taking a chance leaving Abby to guard the money. He still had no idea whether or not she could shoot. But he didn't really have a choice. His place was down here, on the street.

"Any time, gents!" he called out.

Each pair of men looked at each other and then, one-by-one, they turned and left. Now they were hidden, and the game was different.

Clint decided to take the offensive, so he began to move down the street.

***

Abby was back at her window, looking down at the street when she heard something in the hallway. She left the window and went to the door, holding the gun ready. Then she cracked the door and peered into the hall. There was a man in front of Clint's door, with a gun in his hand. He was dressed in well-worn trail clothes.

She swung her door open. "Stand still."

The man froze.

"What do you want?" Abby asked.

"Just the money," the man said, "I don't wanna hurt you."

"I think you should turn and walk away," she told him.

"Ma'am," he said, "you should go back in your room."

"I'm warning you—" she said.

"And I warned you!" he snapped, starting to turn.

She pointed her gun and fired.

***

Clint heard the shot from the hotel. At the same time two men broke from cover and ran across the street toward the livery stable. From the sound of the shot, Clint assumed it had come from Abby's gun. The fact that there was no return shot was encouraging.

As for the two men who had just run to the stable, Clint couldn't take any chances that they wouldn't harm his horse, so he followed.

When he got to the front door, he paused and looked behind him. He saw two men creeping up the street, one on each side. They were hoping to box him inside the stable. Rather than go in, he circled around to the rear.

\*\*\*

Abby looked down at the man she had just killed. Then she heard a sound from down the hall and turned, gun ready.

"Whoa, Ma'am," the desk clerk said, putting his hands out in front of him.

She lowered her weapon.

"Are you all right?" he asked.

"Yes," she said, "but he's not. Help me drag him inside."

The clerk hurried down the hall and together they dragged the man from the hall into Abby's room.

"I want his gun," she said.

The clerk picked the pistol up from the hallway floor and reentered the room. Abby closed the door.

"There may be more," she said, taking the extra gun from him. "I'll have to be ready."

"Do you want me to stay with you, Ma'am?" the clerk asked.

"I think not," she said. "You should go back downstairs and stay safe."

"That is what I hope for you, as well, Ma'am," he said. "Stay safe."

"I'll do my best."

The clerk nodded and left the room.

Abby went back to the window and was concerned when she saw no one in the street.

***

Clint found a small back door in the rear of the livery. He was still hesitant about entering, but also worried about the Tobiano. He wondered if the old hostler was inside.

Then he looked up to the hayloft. The door was open and there was a rope hanging down. The rope could have been there all the time, to aid in hay deliveries, or it had been left there to entice him to climb it, at which time both his hands would be occupied. He would be a sitting duck.

He had three choices; climb the rope; go through the back door; and three, stay where he was and outwait the men. They'd have to come out some time.

He decided to wait.

***

"You said this'd work," one of the men inside said to the other.

"And it will," the second man said. "Just sit tight."

# Chapter Thirty-Four

It had become a waiting game, and Clint was determined to win.

He assumed two of the men were still in the barn, and two were probably out front waiting. Why none of them would think to come to the back, he didn't know. At least there were no more shots coming from the hotel. He assumed Abby was safe for the moment.

There was a buckboard behind the barn, and Clint used it for cover while he waited.

\*\*\*

"What the hell!" one of the men out front said. "Is anybody checking the back? I mean, if he's not inside—"

"Go ahead," the other man said, "check it. I'm gonna stay here."

"I can't believe those two idiots are still inside," the first man said. "Okay, I'll look out back. *Somebody's* got to make a move."

"Somebody did," the other man said. "You heard that shot from the hotel."

"I'll hopefully be right back," the first man said and crossed over to the barn. He kept his back flattened against the wall as he made his way toward the back.

\*\*\*

Clint had to admit he was getting impatient when he saw a man peer around from the side of the barn. Apparently, someone had finally decided to check the back. He could have taken a shot, but he refrained from it. Instead, he made himself visible for just a few seconds, hoping the man would see him and go back and tell his friends.

Once the man's head was withdrawn, Clint changed position and took to the corral, where there were a few horses.

\*\*\*

"He's out back!" the man said, returning to his partner.

"What's he doin', hidin'?" the second man asked.

"Never mind why he's there, he's there," the first man said. "Let's go inside and tell the others, and then we can get this over with."

The two men headed for the barn door.

\*\*\*

Clint figured the four of them would come back there for him. Two might come around the side, and two from the back door. Or one might even go up to the hayloft. However they came, he was ready to make every shot count.

\*\*\*

The four men recruited by Boone were all experienced at hiring their guns out. But in the past, none of them had gone up against someone like the Gunsmith.

"Are we gettin' paid enough for this?" one of them asked, now that they were all inside the livery stable. "I thought we was just gonna shoot it out. This sneakin' around is makin' me nervous."

"We're gettin' paid plenty," another man said. "Okay, one of us goes out the back door, one goes in the hayloft. The other two go outside and come around either side of the barn."

They all agreed.

"Stewie, you sure he's behind the buckboard?" one asked.

"That's where he was when I looked," Stewie said.

"Okay, then, let's go."

The four men split up.

\*\*\*

Clint didn't know if they'd come in twos, or they would split up, but he was prepared for every eventuality. It probably would have been better if he also had his backup gun, the Colt New Line, but he would have to make do with his Peacemaker. It had served him well over the years.

\*\*\*

Abby grew more and more agitated as she heard no shots. She finally made up her mind, grabbed the bag of money from beneath the bed and ran down to the lobby.

"What's your name?" she asked the clerk.

"Ben," he said.

"Ben you have to hide this for me," she said. "And don't look in it. I know it'll be hard, but don't."

"Yes, Ma'am."

"If you and the bag are not here when we get back, the Gunsmith and I will hunt you down. Understand?"

"Yes, Ma'am."

She started away, then turned and said, "If we don't come back, it's yours." Then she ran out.

# Chapter Thirty-Five

Clint saw the first one in the hayloft. The man stuck his head out and peered over at the buckboard, where Clint had been hiding.

Next, the backdoor cracked open, and a man looked out.

Then he saw the other two, on either side of the barn. He knew they were there to kill him, so while he normally never fired the first shot, this was different. His first shot would show them where he was, so it had to count.

The man exposing himself the most was the one in the hayloft. It was an easy shot. He fired, and the man staggered, then fell out all the way to the ground.

The other three made a mistake. Instead of looking to see where the shot had come from, they all looked at their fallen comrade. Clint took the opportunity to holster his gun and step into the open.

"You boys lookin' for me?" Clint asked.

They all turned to face him. Two of them immediately went for their guns. The third—the one who had come out the back door—ran back inside and slammed the door.

Clint drew and fired, killing both men before they could clear leather.

***

The man who ran back inside the barn ran through it to the front door and out. As he came out, he almost ran smack into a woman who was waving a gun.

"Get out of my way!" he snapped.

***

As Abby approached the livery stable, she heard two shots. She stopped in her tracks, and a man came running from the livery stable, almost right into her.

"Get out of my way!" he snapped.

His gun was holstered, while hers was in her hand, so she shot him at point blank range. It was only after she fired the shot that she hoped she had done the right thing.

***

Clint heard the shot from the front of the livery and ran around to see what happened. From the sound of the gun, he thought he knew. When he came to the front, he saw Abby standing with a man lying at her feet. Her gun was still in her hand.

"Are you all right?" he asked.

She stared at him, eyes wide.

"Did I do the right thing?" she asked. "Was he—"

"Yes," Clint said, "he was one of the men sent to kill me. The other three are in the back. What are you doing here?"

"I thought you'd need help," she said.

"What happened at the hotel?"

"They sent a man to your room to look for the money," she said. "I shot him, too."

"And where's the money while you're out here?"

"I gave the bag to the desk clerk to hold."

"And what's he going to do when he sees what's in it?" Clint asked.

"I told him not to look," she said. "And I told him if he and the bag weren't there when we got back, we'd hunt him down."

"Well," Clint said, "let's go and see if your threat worked."

"What about these bodies?" she asked.

"None of our business," Clint said. "Let the town clean up its own mess."

They headed back to the hotel.

***

When they got to the lobby, the desk clerk immediately hauled out the bag and put it on top of the desk.

"There it is, Ma'am," he said, "safe and sound, just like you wanted it."

Clint had never counted the money inside the bag, so he wouldn't have known if a few dollars were missing. He decided if the clerk had snatched some, he had earned it.

"Thank you," Clint said, grabbing the bag. "Now I think there's a mess in . . ." He looked at Abby.

"My room," she said.

". . . Miss West's room to be cleaned up."

"Yes, sir," the clerk said, "I'll have somebody tend to it right away."

"She'll be with me in my room until you do," Clint told him.

"Yes, sir."

"Thank you, Ben," Abby said.

"Yes, Ma'am, you're welcome."

"Ben?" Clint said, as they started up the stairs. "You're on a first name basis with the clerk?"

"I'll bet he doesn't think I'm so plain, anymore," she said.

# Chapter Thirty-Six

They heard someone come down the hall, enter Abby's room, and then the sound of something being dragged. A few minutes later there was a knock at the door. When Clint opened it, the desk clerk was standing there.

"The . . . mess has been cleaned up, Sir," he said.

"Thanks."

"And, uh, the sheriff is downstairs, askin' for you."

"Tell him I'll be right down."

He closed the door.

"What's the sheriff going to do?" Abby asked. "He can't arrest us, can he?"

"He can try."

"We were defending ourselves."

"He knows that," Clint said. "He was watching from his office."

"Watching?" she said. "He was going to let them kill you?"

"Looks like it."

"So what's he want now?" she asked.

"That's what I'm going to find out," he said. "You stay in your room with the money. I'll be right back."

Clint headed for the door, then turned back and pointed his finger at her. "This time I mean it!"

***

When he got down to the lobby, he found an agitated Sheriff Mayhew waiting for him.

"Five men!" Mayhew said. "Five dead men?"

"I only killed three of them," Clint pointed out.

"And your lady friend got the other two," Mayhew said. "I should throw you both in jail."

"You could try, Sheriff," Clint said. "but I wouldn't recommend it."

"So what now?" Mayhew asked.

"Now I keep doing what I've been doing," Clint said. "Looking for Boone and the Tall Texan. I didn't manage to get one of those men alive, but I'm sure they were sent by Boone."

"Did you give them a chance?" Mayhew asked.

"Actually, no, I didn't," Clint said. "I don't give chances to men who have been sent to kill me."

"And you're sure that's what they intended?"

"Oh yeah," Clint said. "Take a look at them, Sheriff. Would-be gunnies, all of them."

"And you just left 'em lyin' there!" Mayhew said.

"You and your town can clean up the mess," Clint said. "After all, you contributed to it."

"Me?"

"You and the whole town, watching the action from your windows," Clint said. "You think I didn't see you?"

Mayhew's face grew red, either from rage or embarrassment, or a combination of both.

"I don't know what to do about you, Adams," he complained.

"I do," Clint said, "just stay out of my way."

"Well," Mayhew said, "somebody's gonna have to do somethin'."

He turned and stormed out of the lobby.

***

Clint ran upstairs and told Abby, "I just got an idea. I'm going to follow the sheriff and see where he takes me."

"But what makes you think he'll lead you anywhere?"

"Something he said," Clint answered. "That somebody has to do something. I think he's going to talk to that somebody."

He left the hotel and headed for the livery stable.

\*\*\*

Sheriff Mayhew left the hotel, went to his office and sat for a few minutes before rising again. He left the office and went to the livery for his horse. Somebody was definitely going to have to do something about the Gunsmith, and he knew who that someone would have to be.

\*\*\*

As Clint entered the livery, the old hostler put his hands out and said, "I didn't have nothin' to do with them varmints. I hid in the back when they come in."

"I believe you," Clint said. "Did the sheriff come and get his horse?"

"He did, yeah," the man said, "a few minutes ago."

"What's he riding?"

"A dun."

"Show me where it was."

The hostler took Clint to an empty stall. Clint examined the ground, studying and memorizing the hoof prints the dun had left.

"Okay," Clint said, "I'm going to saddle my horse. You can relax."

# Chapter Thirty-Seven

Clint picked up the dun's trail just outside of town. He had no idea where the sheriff was going, but he was determined to follow him all the way. His abilities as a tracker had improved over the years, and he was quite sure he would be able to track the man to his destination.

\*\*\*

Sheriff Mayhew rode to Tonka and reined in his horse in front of the trading post. He went inside, found the white-haired owner standing behind the counter. There were no customers in the place.

"Sheriff," the man said. "What brings you here?"

"Five dead men," Mayhew said.

"What?"

"Your son and Boone sent five men after the Gunsmith," Mayhew said. "They're all dead."

The man did not look directly at the lawman.

"Why tell me?"

"Somebody has to do something about the Gunsmith," Mayhew said.

"You're the law."

"I'm not a gunman," Mayhew said. "My badge is no match for his gun. We need the Tall Texan to come and handle this, himself."

"Your whole town only exists because of him," the man said. "You can't handle one man for him? I've told him how foolish this relationship is. Maybe now he'll listen to me and leave you on your own."

"He considers Woodriver his home," Mayhew said.

"And I don't know why," the man said. "His home is here, with me."

"In Tonka? This ain't even a town."

"Not in Tonka," the man said, "with me, his father."

"All right," Mayhew said, "just tell 'im I was here. Let him make up his own mind."

Grudgingly, the man said, "I'll tell 'im."

"Thanks."

Mayhew left, mounted his horse and headed back to Woodriver. He figured he'd make it by nightfall.

***

Clint tracked the sheriff to Tonka, figured he was still there, so he waited. He saw a horse in front of the trading post, eventually the sheriff came out and rode away, apparently back toward Woodriver. Clint let him go. He had what he wanted.

When Mayhew was out of sight, Clint rode into Tonka and stopped in front of the trading post. He dismounted, looked around the dismal excuse for a town, and then entered.

The man behind the counter was white-haired, in his sixties. As with the store in Woodriver, this one sold supplies or drinks.

"What can I do for you, friend?" the man asked.

"Whiskey," Clint said, because he saw no beer taps.

"Right away."

The man poured Clint a shot, which he tossed back quickly.

"Another?" the man asked.

"No, thank you," Clint said. "I need to talk to Boone, or the Tall Texan."

"Texan?" the man said. "I don't know what you mean."

"Yeah, you do," Clint said. "I saw Sheriff Mayhew leave. I followed him here from Woodriver. He told you about the five dead men."

The man remained silent. He was quite a tall man, probably around six-four, but Clint felt he was too old to be the Texan, himself.

"You're his father," he said suddenly.

"What are you talkin' about," the man said. "I run a trading post. That's all."

"Go ahead," Clint said, "deny that you're the Tall Texan's father."

The man didn't speak.

"You can't deny him, can you?"

Suddenly, recognition dawned on the man.

"You're him," he said, almost in awe. "You're Clint Adams, the Gunsmith."

"That's right."

"You're here to kill him."

"No," Clint said, "I'm here to catch him, and take him to court for his crimes."

"That's not what you do."

"How do you know what I do?" Clint demanded.

"I know your reputation."

"You know his, too," Clint said. "All true?"

The man hesitated, then said, "No."

"Then tell me where he is," Clint said, "and we'll find out whose reputation is true or not."

The old man stared at Clint, then said, "Have another drink."

# Chapter Thirty-Eight

The old man poured Clint another shot, then walked to the front door, locked it and got back behind the counter. Then he poured himself a drink. He didn't speak until he had tossed it off and poured a second.

"I've told him he's gonna get himself killed," he said, "but do kids listen to their parents?"

Clint didn't answer. He hadn't raised any kids, never would, so he was no authority.

"So I'm right? The Tall Texan is your son," Clint said.

"Tall Texan," the old man said. "What a stupid name. My son's name is Travis Buckle. He didn't pick that Texan name, you know. Some stupid newspaperman gave it to him, and it stuck."

"I know how he feels," Clint said.

"Yeah, I suppose you would," the old man said, pouring two more drinks.

"What's your name?" Clint asked.

"I'm William Buckle," the man said. "Don't call me Bill."

"I'll call you Mr. Buckle," Clint said. "Where's your son, Mr. Buckle?"

"I can't tell you that," he said. "You'll kill 'im."

"I'm not looking to kill him," Clint said. "As far as I know, he hasn't killed anybody. But I am looking to bring him in. If he's not stopped, he's eventually going to have to kill somebody during a robbery."

"You're sayin' he's gonna kill somebody," Buckle said, "and I'm tellin' him he's gonna get killed."

"And I'm trying to prevent both of those things," Clint told him.

"I can't betray my boy," Buckle said.

"Okay, then, tell me who Boone is and why he's involved?"

"Boone's Travis' cousin, my brother's boy," Buckle said. "He lived with us for a while growin' up after his Pa died."

"So when Travis started this business of stealing money—" Clint began.

"He steals it and gives it to Boone, who takes it to town and spreads it out. Without Travis, Woodriver woulda dried up years ago."

"And why is he doing that?" Clint asked.

"Because he's a good boy, and because he considers Woodriver his home," Buckle said. "I keep tellin' him his home's here with me."

"Tell me something," Clint said. "Was this all Travis' idea?"

"If you ask Travis he'd say yes," the old man said, "but I blame the whole thing on the bank manager, Cooke."

"The bank manager is in on it?"

"Right in the middle," Buckle said. "I believe the whole thing was his idea. Honest, Mr. Adams, I did try to stop him from stealin'."

"I believe you, Sir," Clint said. "He's obviously got a mind of his own."

"Oh, yeah, he does have that," Buckle said.

"How old is he?"

"He's barely twenty-five," Buckle said.

"Still young enough to have a lot of life ahead of him," Clint said.

"I hope so."

"So where can I find Boone?"

"Mr. Adams," Buckle said, "you just told me that Boone sent five men to kill you. If I tell you where he is, *you'll* kill *him*. How could I live with that?"

"How are you going to live with your son eventually being killed?" Clint asked.

That made Buckle pour himself another drink.

"You gotta let me talk to my boy," he said. "Maybe I can get him to give himself up. Or at least meet with ya."

"Can you do that today?"

"I dunno," Buckle said, honestly. "Today or tomorrow."

"And can you keep Boone from sending any more men after me?"

"I can do that," Buckle said.

Clint looked past Buckle at the curtained doorway in the rear wall.

"If I go into that back room, am I going to find Boone or your son there?"

"They do meet there," Buckle said, "but ain't neither of them there now."

Clint stared at the doorway a little longer, then looked back at the older man.

"All right, Mr. Buckle," he said. "I'll be in Woodriver until I get this done. I hope I hear from you, or Boone, or your son."

"I'll tell them," Buckle said.

"And tell your son if he comes in, it'd be easier if he came in unarmed."

"And you ain't gonna kill 'im?"

"I'm not going to kill him," Clint said. "I'll take him in, he'll be tried and will do some time, but he'll still have a lot of years ahead of him when he gets out."

"I'll do my best, Mr. Adams."

Clint nodded, backed his way toward the door, and left. As the old man heard Clint's horse galloping away, Travis came through the curtained doorway.

"You shoulda let him back, Pa," he said. "I woulda shot 'im."

"You ain't killed anybody in your life, Travis," Buckle said, "why start now?"

"Well, it's like he said, Pa," Travis answered. "It's gotta happen sooner or later."

"No, it don't," Buckle said. "Just forget about all this and give yerself up, boy."

"Pa, you did a real fine job of convincing him you want me to stop. You don't have to try and convince me."

"But I *do* want you to stop," Buckle said. "In fact, I never wanted you to start. You let that damned bank manager talk you into this."

"Mr. Cooke?" Travis said. "He don't run me, Pa. I'm callin' all the shots here, I'm the Tall Texan, remember?"

"It's gonna get real dangerous if you start believin' in your own reputation, boy."

"What's not to believe?" he asked. "Nobody's been able to stop me, yet."

"And now you got the Gunsmith after you."

"Not for long," Travis said.

"Whatayou got in mind?"

"I'm gonna do like he said," Travis answered. "I'm gonna ride into Woodriver."

The old man's white eyebrows went up.

"Unarmed?" he asked.

"Hell, no, Pa," Travis said, "how am I gonna kill the Gunsmith if I'm unarmed?"

# Chapter Thirty-Nine

Clint rode back to Woodriver and arrived after dark. As he unsaddled his horse he wondered if he had done the right thing by not going into that back room. If he'd gone, the whole matter might have come to an end. There was a good chance Travis Buckle was back there, but now he was going to have to keep waiting.

The old man had seemed sincere. He was going to talk to his son, but that didn't mean Travis would listen. But just because Clint had to wait and see what happened didn't mean he'd be idle while he waited. The new information he had about the bank manager needed his attention. So in the morning, when the bank opened, he was going to be there. Imagine a bank manager planning a robbery of his own bank. He wondered if the townspeople knew about that part of the grand plan?

He walked the dark, empty street to his hotel, eyes and ears alert for an ambush. It would probably take Boone a while to recruit a new group of gunnies, but there was no harm in being careful.

He made it to the lobby without anyone taking a shot at him. The clerk watched as he crossed the floor.

"Anybody looking for me, Ben?"

"No, Sir."

"Is Miss West in her room?"

"She ain't come down since you left," the clerk said.

"Good," Clint said. "'night, then."

"Good night, Sir."

Clint went up the stairs and stopped in front of Abby's door. She opened the door as soon as he knocked, gave him a quick hug and pulled him inside.

"Oh my God, I've been so worried," she said. "Where did you go?"

"A small town near here called Tonka," he said, and went on to tell her the conversation he had with William Buckle.

"Tonka, Texas?" she said. "I never heard of it."

"It's a mud puddle," Clint said. "But it's where Boone and the Texan come together."

"And they were there now? You met the Texan?

Clint hesitated.

"Clint?"

"One of them may have been in the back room," he said, "but I agreed to let Mr. Buckle talk to his son, try to get him to give himself up."

"And do you think he will?"

"Surrender? I'm thinking no. He's a young man, and he seems to have bought into his reputation. But I wanted to give the old man a chance."

"I didn't know you had such a big heart," she said.

"Well, don't tell anybody," Clint said.

"So you expect him to come in and face you?"

"He might," Clint said. "He might come in with Boone, or they might send in some more guns. We just have to wait and see."

"More waiting?" she said, scowling. "I'm getting so impatient."

"If you plan to stay in this business, you're going to have to learn to wait," Clint told her.

"Maybe it'll get easier the older I get," Abby said.

"Well, start working on it now," he said. "I'm going to my room to sleep."

"Really?" Abby asked. "I thought—"

"I know what you thought," he said, "but we both have to be careful and alert. We can't afford to let ourselves be distracted."

"I'm a distraction?" she asked.

"Definitely," he said. "Good night."

He left and went to his room before she could do anything to change his mind.

# Chapter Forty

The night passed peacefully, which suited Clint just fine. The day before had brought too many dead men. He dressed and knocked on Abby's door.

"Breakfast?" he asked.

"I'm starving."

They went down to the small dining room again and ate a big breakfast together. From their table they could see if anyone entered the hotel from the front. Just to be on the safe side, they took the bag of money with them and put it on the floor beneath the table.

"What now?" she asked. "Wait, don't tell me. More waiting."

"If I take you with me, we'll have to carry this bag with us," Clint said.

"We could give it to Ben, at the desk," Abby said. "He watched it before."

"And why tempt him, again?" Clint said. "Besides, I'm not convinced he didn't take a few dollars for his trouble."

"He's a sweet boy," she argued. "He wouldn't steal from me."

"This whole town is dealing in stolen money, Abby," Clint said. "You think he's any different?"

"So you want me to stay here and guard the money," she said, shoulders slumped.

"That's right."

"Why don't we just put it in the bank?" she asked.

He reminded her of what he had told her the night before about the bank manager.

"Oh, that's right," she said. "I'm not awake yet. Not thinking straight."

"So, you go back to your room, and I'll go to the bank," he said, as they stood up. "With any luck, Buckle will come riding in this morning."

They left the dining room together and Clint watched as Abby walked across the lobby and up the stairs. When she was out of sight, he left the hotel and headed for the bank.

*** 

The small bank was empty but for the two employees. They both recognized him from his last visit. The woman remained at her desk as he approached the man behind the cage.

"Mr. Adams," the man said. "What can we do for you this morning?"

"I'd like to see Mr. Cooke," Clint said. "Is he in?"

"Yes, sir," he said. "I'll let him know you're here."

Clint waited and eventually the teller took him to Cooke's office.

"Mr. Adams," Cooke said from behind his desk. "What brings you here?"

"Money," Clint said.

"Do you need to borrow some?" the man asked. "Or deposit some?"

"If I was going to deposit my money in a bank, it wouldn't be here, Mr. Cooke," Clint said.

"I'm sorry to hear that."

"Do you know why I say that?" Clint asked.

"I'm afraid I don't."

"Because I can't trust a bank manager who would rob his own bank."

Cooke sat back in his chair.

"And why would you say that?"

"You worked with Travis Buckle to rob this bank," Clint said. "Got him started on the road to becoming the Tall Texan."

"Where did you get this information?" Cooke asked. "It's preposterous."

"I spoke with William Buckle," Clint said. "You can't deny any of this, Cooke. Travis robs banks, trains and whatever and then sends the money back here. His cousin Boone and you distribute the money around town. This entire town is existing on stolen money."

"Look," Cooke said, "it was all Travis' idea—"

"Really?" Clint said. "He came up with the idea back when he was twenty years old? And you just went along with it?"

"The entire town was in trouble," Cooke said. "Including this bank."

"Well," Clint said, "you all should've moved on. Instead, this kid has become a wanted man. So why don't you tell me where he is?"

"What? I don't know that," Cooke said. "You say you spoke with his father. Why don't you ask him?"

"I did," Clint said. "Now I'm asking you. When's the last time you saw him?"

"Oh, it was a long time ago," Cooke said. "He never comes here."

"And Boone?" Clint asked. "When did you see him?"

"A couple of days ago," Cooke said. "He comes and goes."

"And where does he live?"

"That I don't know," Cooke said. "He keeps that to himself."

"So what do you know?"

"Nothing," Cooke said, flapping his arms. "You've got the wrong idea about me."

"I don't think so, Mr. Cooke," Clint said. "This all kind of makes sense with you involved."

Cooke laughed.

"Do you think I'm some sort of criminal mastermind?"

"That could very well be what you are," Clint said. "Whatever your involvement is, Mr. Cooke, I'm going to root it out."

"Mr. Adams," Cooke said, "are you trying to ruin this town?"

"I don't think I could," Clint said. "I think all you folks did that a long time ago."

He turned and left before Cooke could offer any sort of reply.

\*\*\*

After Clint left the bank manager's office, Cooke sat there in a state of panic. He wasn't worried about losing his job, or about the town going under, he was worried about losing all the money he had personally made over the past four years. He decided it might be time for him to simply pack up and leave town very quietly.

# Chapter Forty-One

Nobody in town knew where Jason Boone lived, but his cousin Travis Buckle did. Travis rode from Tonka to his cousin's house, dismounted and approached the door, the lower portion of his face covered with a bandana. He didn't do that to hide his identity from his cousin, he did it to let him know this was Tall Texan business.

The house was the one Boone had grown up in, and it was now rundown due to neglect. People in town would have been surprised to realize Boone still lived there.

Travis knocked on the door and kept knocking until a bleary-eyed Boone opened it.

"What the hell are you doin' here?" he asked. The only place he'd seen his cousin over the past four years was in Tonka.

"Business, Jace," he said. "Let me in."

Boone backed up to allow Travis to enter. The inside was bare except for a pot-bellied stove, a rickety table with one chair, and a sagging bed.

"How can you live here?" Travis asked. "You've got the money to fix this place."

"It's fine," Boone said. "What brings you here?"

"Your five men didn't get the job done," Travis said. "And Adams came to see my Pa."

"How the hell did he find your Pa?"

"He followed the sheriff."

"Jesus," Boone said, "so he knows who you are? What do we do now?"

"We're gonna have to take care of him ourselves," Travis said.

"Go up against the Gunsmith?" Boone said, swallowing hard.

"Don't worry," Travis said, "I can take him. I just need you to back my play."

"When?" Boone asked.

"Today," Travis said. "Let's get this done so we can go on with our business. But first we'll have to go and see Cooke."

"You think Adams knows about him?"

"I think Adams thinks he knows everythin'," Travis said. "What we're gonna show 'im is that he don't know nothin', at all!"

\*\*\*

Clint wondered if, after he left town, Woodriver's populace would come out onto the street? He hadn't seen more than two or three people walking about the whole time he'd been there.

Leaving the bank Clint figured he had talked to everybody he could. Now it was up to Travis Buckle to do something. He could run and hide, or he could come out into the open. If he did that, he could surrender, or fight. Clint walked to the hotel, where there were a few chairs out front. He grabbed one and settled into it to wait. Like he told Abby, you had to be patient. He had poked his nose everywhere he could possibly poke it. Now it was about the waiting.

***

Henry Cooke looked up when his office door opened. He hoped it wasn't Clint Adams, again. He still hadn't made his final decision about what to do. He relaxed when he saw Travis Buckle and Jason Boone enter.

"Did you come in the back?" he asked.

"Of course," Travis said. "Nobody saw us."

"Take that bandana off your face," Cooke said, "I know who you are."

Travis yanked the bandana down so that it settled around his neck.

"Why are you here?" Cooke demanded.

"Clint Adams came to see my Pa," Travis said. "It's time for me to come out in the open and see 'im."

"If he kills you, this town will die, too," Cooke said.

"He ain't gonna kill me, Cooke," Travis said. "Has he come to see you?"

"Yes," Cooke said, "twice. Second time was just this morning. Look, if you take care of him, we can keep going on as before. If not, I'm afraid it's all over."

"Well," Travis said, "we'll see about that. Jace and me, we're gonna go and see 'im."

"I wish you luck, then," Cooke said.

Travis looked at his cousin and said, "Let's go and see what the man has to say."

He pulled the bandana up over the lower part of his face again, and they left the office.

\*\*\*

After the two men left the bank Cooke got an idea. He came to the decision, if the outcome of the day was going to affect the entire town, then why not get the whole town involved? He put on his hat and jacket and rushed out of the bank.

# Chapter Forty-Two

Clint saw the two men walking toward him. He recognized Boone, saw the bandana across the face of the tall man next to him. He had the feeling folks were peering out their windows, again.

He remained seated, watching the two men walk. The tall one—apparently the Tall Texan—had a holstered pistol on his right hip. Boone had a gun tucked into his belt. He wasn't going to be much of a problem.

As they approached him, Clint could see that Boone was very nervous. He couldn't gauge Travis Buckle's attitude, not with that mask covering his face. As they got closer, he saw that Buckle was at least six-foot-five in his boots. He was a Tall Texan, indeed.

"Clint Adams?" the masked man asked.

"That's right."

"I hear you been lookin for me."

"That depends on who you are," Clint said.

"Ain't this a clue?" the man asked, pointing to the mask.

"Anybody can wear a mask," Clint said.

"My name's Travis Buckle," the man said. "You talked to my Pa yesterday."

"Anybody could know that, too."

"This is my cousin Boone," the man said. "He'll tell you who I am."

Clint looked at Boone.

"It's him, all right," Boone said. "Travis is the Tall Texan."

"Well," Clint said, "you're tall, that's for sure."

The tall man frowned.

"Hey, whatsatta with you?" he asked. "You been lookin' all over for me, talkin' to folks, botherin' my Pa. Now I tell ya here I am, and you don't believe me?"

"Well," Clint said, "the Tall Texan has quite a reputation. You just seem a little young to me. Why don't you take off the mask?"

The tall man frowned, then tugged the mask down from his face. Clint wouldn't have called him handsome, but he was pleasant looking enough and young.

"Well, hell," Clint said, "you don't even shave yet, do you?"

The man frowned and put his hand to his jaw before he could stop himself.

"Mister," he said, dropping his hand, "I robbed trains, banks, stagecoaches, stores . . . I done everything they say I done."

"So are you here to turn yourself in?" Clint asked. He knew he had the young man off balance, and he wanted to keep him that way.

"Not exactly."

"Well, I can't say I'm convinced," Clint said. "Some men just want to claim a reputation, even if it isn't theirs."

The young man firmed his jaw and looked puzzled.

"Anybody in this town can tell you who I am," he claimed.

"Well, that's not exactly true."

"Whataya mean?"

"The Tall Texan keeps his face covered," Clint said. "Folks hereabouts claim they don't know exactly who he is."

"What the—" The young man looked at Boone, who shrugged. Then he looked back at Clint. "You stay right there. Don't you move."

"I got no place to go," Clint said.

The two young men turned and walked away. Clint smiled at their retreating backs.

\*\*\*

"What the hell are ya doin', Travis?" Boone asked, as they walked away. "I thought you was gonna kill 'im."

"When I kill 'im," Travis said, "I want him to know who I am."

# Chapter Forty-Three

When Travis and Boone entered the sheriff's office, Mayhew was surprised. Travis had pulled up his mask.

"What the hell—" he said.

"Mayhew," Travis said, "I need you tell Clint Adams that I'm the Tall Texan."

"Why do you want me to do that?"

"Because I intend to kill the Gunsmith," Travis said, "and I want him to know it's me."

"Take off that silly mask," Mayhew said.

Travis pulled it down.

"You think if I tell Adams you're the Texan he'll believe me?"

"Yeah, I do."

"And why's that matter?"

"You know why," Travis said. "So I can keep doin' what I'm doin'."

"That's why you need to kill 'im," Mayhew said. "It's not why you feel he needs to know who you are."

"He's a legend," Travis said. "He deserves to know who is killin' him."

"Okay then, I'll let him know."

"When?"

"This afternoon."

"Why not now?" Travis asked.

"Because before you got here, Mr. Cooke was in," Mayhew said.

"What did he want?"

"He had an idea," Mayhew said.

"What was it?"

"Have a seat and I'll tell you . . ."

\*\*\*

Clint sat and waited. Travis Buckle had not returned. Apparently, something was delaying him.

"Clint?"

He turned and saw Abby standing in the doorway.

"What are you doing out of your room?"

"I'm hungry," she said. "Come in and have something to eat with me."

"The Texan was here," Clint said. "I'm waiting for him to come back."

"If he looks for you," she said, "he'll find you in the dining room."

She had a point. And he was feeling hungry.

"All right, Abby." He stood and followed her inside.

\*\*\*

"You think this'll work?" Travis asked Mayhew after the lawman had told him Cooke's plans.

"I think it might keep you from gettin' killed," Sheriff Mayhew said. "And it might even keep you from killin' the Gunsmith."

"Just why would I not wanna kill him?"

"You're a young man, Travis," Mayhew said. "Killing the Gunsmith will paint a target on your back for the rest of your life. You don't wanna do that. This way is better."

Travis looked at Boone, who simply shrugged.

"When will this be arranged?" Travis asked.

"Later this afternoon," Mayhew said, "before dusk. When the sun goes down, we'd like this all to be over."

***

Clint and Abby had steaks, with all the trimmings. It reminded him of when she had ordered the food in San Francisco. Once again she ate quickly, with her arms around her plate. Once again, the bag of recovered money was under the table.

"You're eating like it's your last meal," he said.

"I'm afraid I may be eating your last meal with you," she said. "Why would you be sitting out front of the hotel, waiting to be shot?"

"It's just a way to draw the Texan out," he said. "And it worked."

"You have to let me sit with you," she said.

"Not a chance."

"You know I can shoot," she insisted. "I've killed two men."

"I know you have, and that's more than I wanted you to do," he said. "After you finish eating, you take that bag back to your room and stay there. Keep your gun ready. And don't open the door for anyone but me."

"I know," she said, "you told me all that before."

"And yet you still came out of your room," he said. "Twice."

"Clint—"

"Stay put, Abby," he said. "This will all be over soon, and I'll be sure to tell Robert Pinkerton that a lot of the credit is yours. Deal?"

"Deal."

# Chapter Forty-Four

After supper Clint sent Abby up to her room and went back out front to sit. It was dusk, not far from darkness falling. If Travis Buckle was going to try something, it should be soon. Clint had only been trying to confuse him with all that talk about who he was and had apparently succeeded.

It didn't take long for Travis Buckle and Boone to appear, and they once again walked toward him. Only this time they stopped in the center of the street.

"Okay, Adams," Travis said from behind the mask he had pulled up again, "step out here, and we'll get it done."

Clint stood up.

"Is this really the way you want this to end, Travis?" Clint asked. "I promised your father I'd try not to kill you."

"Don't worry," Travis said, "I'll make sure you keep that promise."

Clint could see very clearly that Boone was sweating.

"How does your cousin feel about this?" he asked.

"He feels just fine," Travis said. "Now step on out here and don't keep me waitin'."

Clint stepped down into the street, moved out to the center to face the two young men.

"I only wanted to bring you in, Travis," he said. "I didn't want this."

"Well, I guess you got more than you bargained for, then," Travis said.

Suddenly, Clint felt a change in the landscape. Doors began to open, and people began to come out. He noticed several storekeepers holding rifles, and more doors opened, and more armed citizens began to appear. Before long, he and the two young men were surrounded by an armed citizenry. He was pretty sure they weren't there to back him against their savior, the Tall Texan.

"Looks like you've got help," Clint said to Travis.

"Looks like," Travis said.

One man stepped forward, and Clint saw that it was Sheriff Mayhew.

"The people of this town ain't gonna let you kill 'im, Adams," he said. "You'd be killin' the town, too."

"You people killed your own town a long time ago, when you started accepting stolen money."

A murmur went through the crowd. They didn't like being told that. Clint looked around, was surprised to see that some of the armed people were women.

"Travis, you really want to turn all these decent people into killers?" Clint asked.

"They're standin' up for their town, Adams," Travis said. "This is self-defense."

Clint looked around again. More than half the people seemed scared.

"How many of them do you really think will use their weapons?" he asked.

"It'll only take one," Sheriff Mayhew said.

"Well, Sheriff," Clint said, "before they kill me, I'll kill you first, and Travis second. Neither one of you will see the outcome of this stand-off."

Mayhew looked shaken by that.

"Don't let 'im scare you, Sheriff," Travis said. "We gotta stand up to him. You told me this was your idea."

"This was Cooke's idea," Mayhew said, "but I ain't sure I wanna see it through."

"That's fine, then," Travis said. "Step aside and let me and the townspeople do your job for ya."

"I don't think so, Travis," Clint said. "I can already see some of these guns getting heavy in their hands."

Sure enough, some of the rifle barrels were starting to droop and point to the ground. But there were still enough to do damage.

"You folks should go back into your shops and homes," Clint said. "Let your Tall Texan take care of his own business."

Travis looked around, and Clint could see some doubt creeping into his face.

The people just needed one little push.

\*\*\*

Staring out her window, Abby could see what was happening. They had managed to turn the whole town against Clint, and they were out there on the street with guns in their hands. She knew she had to do something to help.

She grabbed the bag of money and ran from the room.

\*\*\*

Clint was wondering what the push would be when suddenly Abby came bursting from the hotel.

"Wait! Wait!" she shouted.

All heads turned to her. She ran into the center of the street, stood between Clint and Travis. She threw the sack of money down. Cash spilled onto the street.

The sheriff had moved to one side. Now he stared at the money, then back at Clint.

# Chapter Forty-Five

"You folks all think that the Tall Texan and Henry Cooke have been distributing the stolen money among you but look there. This is a cache of money we found hidden in the floorboards of a line shack outside of town. It's money they've been saving for themselves."

The people all looked at the bag of money, and then at Travis Buckle.

"I—I don't know where that money came from," Travis called out. "I—I've got nothin' to do with that."

People began talking to each other, and then slowly drifting back off the street and indoors.

"Hey!" Travis shouted. "Where you goin'? This ain't over."

"It's over for them, Travis," Clint said. "Now it's you, Boone, and the sheriff."

"Oh, hey," Sheriff Mayhew said, putting his hands in the air, "I got no part in this. Travis, if you, Cooke and Boone have been stealin', this is all your doin'."

The sheriff waved both his hands and walked away.

"Stealing," Clint said. "That's funny. You've been stealing stolen money, Travis."

Clint waved one hand at Abby, and she retreated to the front of the hotel.

"All right, Travis," Clint said. "Let's make your reputation . . . or break it."

"Travis . . ." Boone said.

"Don't back out on me now, Jace."

"It's all over, Travis," Boone said. "I don't wanna die here in the street like a dog."

Travis turned away from Clint and looked at his cousin.

"Where'd this money come from, Jace?" he asked, pointing at the bag.

"Th-that's Cooke's doin'," Boone said. "He's the one who told me to hold some money out for us."

"Us?" Travis said.

"Well, sure," Boone said. "We was gonna cut you in, Travis."

Travis stared at his cousin, then pulled his bandana down from his face and looked at Clint.

"I'm done, Adams," he said, "but I'm bettin' Cooke's got some money in his private safe, in his office."

"Okay," Clint said. "Why don't we go and check?"

***

When Clint and Travis entered the bank, Boone remained outside. The teller and the clerk both stared at them with wide eyes.

"Where's Cooke?" Travis asked.

"He—he went out the back door," the teller said.

"When?" Clint asked.

"Just a few minutes ago."

"Did he have anything with him?" Clint asked.

"Yes," the teller said, "a bank bag."

Clint and Travis looked at each other.

"The livery stable," Travis said, and they both left the bank.

\*\*\*

Henry Cooke, in the face of everything that was happening in the street, had decided not to await the outcome. It was time for him to make his escape. He took the money from his private safe, stashed it in a bank bag, and went out the back door. He stayed to the back alleys, waiting to hear gunshots from the street. Eventually, he made it to the livery stable and started to hitch up his horse to his buggy. The hostler had left to watch the activity in the street.

As Cooke climbed onto the seat and picked up the reins, the money bag next to him, he wondered why there had been no shots, yet?

\*\*\*

As Clint and Travis reached the livery, with Boone lagging behind, Harry Cooke came out, driving his buggy. He reined his horse in when he saw them.

"Hold it, Cooke!" Travis yelled.

Clint stood next to Travis, holding the bag of money in his left hand. Travis pointed to it.

"I think you forgot somethin', Cooke," Travis said. "Your share."

"What are you doing, Travis?" Cooke demanded. "I was just getting ready to give you a ride out of town."

"It's all over, Cooke," Clint said. "Your skimming of already stolen money all these years is over."

"Are you going to listen to him, Travis?" Cooke asked. "After we've been partners?"

"What about that money bag next to you, Cooke?" Travis asked.

"Your share is in there, Travis."

"I don't want a share," Travis said. "All the money was supposed to go to the town."

"Don't tell me you think I've been keeping some of it?" Cooke asked.

"That's what Boone told me, Cooke," Travis said. "And from what I've seen today, I believe 'im."

"Goddamnit, Travis!" Cooke yelled. "We deserve some of this money."

"No we don't, Cooke," Travis said. "Get down from that buggy before I blast you off it."

Cooke stared at the younger man, then reluctantly climbed down. Travis walked over, grabbed the bag of money, then handed it to Clint. Then he looked past Clint at Boone, who had caught up.

"Any more, Jace?" he asked.

"Yeah," Boone said, "there's some under the floorboards of the line shack."

"You hid it there, again?" Travis asked.

"I didn't think anybody would look there, again."

Travis looked at Clint.

"He might've been right," Clint admitted.

"You go get that money, Jace, and bring it to the hotel," Travis said.

"All of it?" Boone asked.

"Yeah, Jace," Travis said. "All of it."

# Chapter Forty-Six

The next morning Clint and Abby had breakfast together in the hotel. Travis, Boone and Cooke were all in jail. Clint had convinced Mayhew to do his job, for a change.

"Do you think Cooke and Boone will be charged?" Abby asked.

"I don't know," Clint said. "Travis has done all the robberies. Boone and Cooke handled a lot of the stolen money. My guess is they'll be charged with something."

"Where are we going to take them?" she asked. "Not to San Francisco."

"I'm not turning them over to Pinkerton," Clint said. "We'll go to the closest town with a telegraph, and then I'll contact the federal marshals. Let them send somebody to come and get them."

"Will you be coming back to San Francisco, then?"

"No," Clint said, "you can tell Pinkerton what happened, and take as much or as little credit as you want."

"I'll take just enough," she said. "But I'll tell him what you did."

"That's fine," Clint said.

"When will we be leaving?" she asked.

"Right after breakfast," he said. "I've had about as much of Woodriver as I can take."

"I couldn't agree with you more," she said.

# Coming May 27, 2021

## Save $2.00 Pre-order Today!

# THE GUNSMITH

## 470

## Gunsmith for Hire

## For more information
## visit: www.SpeakingVolumes.us

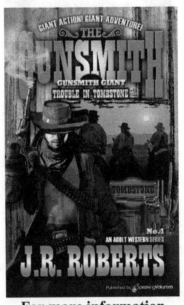

# On Sale Now!

**Lady Gunsmith** *series*
**Books 1 - 9**
**Roxy Doyle and the Lady Executioner**

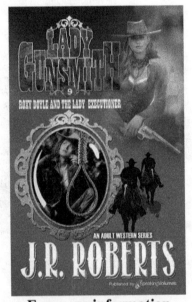

**For more information**
visit:

# On Sale Now!

## Award-Winning Author
## Robert J. Randisi (J.R. Roberts)

## For more information
**visit:** www.SpeakingVolumes.us